Words That Start With B

by VIKKI VANSICKLE

Scholastic Canada Ltd.
Toronto New York London Auckland Sydney
Mexico City New Delhi Hong Kong Buenos Aires

For My Parents

Scholastic Canada Ltd.
604 King Street West, Toronto, Ontario M5V 1E1, Canada

Scholastic Inc.
557 Broadway, New York, NY 10012, USA

Scholastic Australia Pty Limited
PO Box 579, Gosford, NSW 2250, Australia

Scholastic New Zealand Limited
Private Bag 94407, Botany, Manukau 2163, New Zealand

Scholastic Children's Books
Euston House, 24 Eversholt Street, London NW1 1DB, UK

Library and Archives Canada Cataloguing in Publication
VanSickle, Vikki, 1982-
Words that start with B / Vikki VanSickle.
ISBN 978-1-4431-0235-3
I. Title.
PS8643.A59W67 2010   jC813'.6   C2010-901826-5

Cover image: bodhihill/istockphoto

6 5 4 3 2 1   Printed in Canada 121   10 11 12 13 14 15

Before

In grade seven your life is supposed to change forever. At least, it does if you're a student at Ferndale Public School. That's the year you spend in Miss Ross's class, if you're lucky. If you're not, you end up in 7A with Mrs. White and spend the whole year wishing you were in Miss Ross's class. The kids in 7A pretend they don't care, saying the A stands for A+, but you can just as easily say that the B in 7B stands for better or best, and that would be the truth. There is no reason why some kids end up in 7A and some in 7B; it's just one of those cosmic mystical things that is decided by the universe. I hope I'm on her good side this year.

Benji

I'm not the only one who loves Miss Ross. Ferndale students spend their entire lives waiting to be in her class. She always does the coolest stuff. Last year her students adopted a whale, and they decorated the display case in the front hall with pictures of it and facts on whales and how they are becoming endangered. Or some of them are. I don't remember exactly what the reports said because mostly I was looking at the pictures. They adopted a beluga whale named Aurora. Beluga whales are totally white and they look like they are always smiling. I guess no one told them about the icebergs melting and all the oil spills that are wrecking the environment.

The year before that Miss Ross's class planted a school garden where the old playground used to be before they tore it down because it was unsafe. They turned an old muddy patch of land into a wild flower garden, complete with a bird bath and a pathway to walk on. Miss Ross was always doing things like that. And now I was finally in grade seven and about to be in Miss Ross's class — I hoped. What sort of project would my class be taking on? Maybe she was planning it right now. Maybe she was staying up late, putting the finishing touches on a big presentation.

I could hardly wait for next week to come.

There is only one person in the whole world who is feeling as anxious as I am right now. He just so happens to be my best friend. The phone barely rings before it's picked up.

"Hello?"

"Benji?"

"Hi Clarissa."

"What do you think Miss Ross is planning for us this year?"

"I don't know. I guess we'll find out on Tuesday."

"Well I can't wait that long."

"What are you going to do?"

"I was thinking maybe we could call the school."

"Why?"

"To ask Miss Ross."

There is a long pause, which means Benji is trying to find a way to say he thinks I am crazy. I have known him for five years and I know what every single one of his pauses means.

"What would you say?" he finally asks.

"I don't know; maybe I could pretend to be a parent and just ask."

"Why couldn't you just ask her as yourself?"

Honestly. That Benji. I explain myself as patiently as possible, which I admit isn't very patient. "*Because* teachers never tell kids that kind of stuff. They want us to wait and see. But I bet she'd tell a parent. Teachers are obligated to tell parents that kind of thing."

"But won't she recognize your voice?"

"Not if I disguise it," I point out.

Benji is not convinced.

"I guess," he says.

"So are you going to come over?"

"Now?"

"Yes, now. We have to practise the phone call if we want it to sound good."

"We?"

"I'm hanging up now, Benji."

"Okay, I'm coming."

***

Benji has lived next door for as long as I have lived here, but I never really noticed him until the day his father dragged him over to get his hair trimmed and forgot about him. He said he was going to run an errand, and one errand turned into three and then he met some friends for lunch downtown at Good Times. So Benji stayed over for the rest of the day. Before that he was just the weird, skinny kid who stared out the window but never came outside, and who scurried to school in the mornings, like maybe if he moved fast enough no one would see him.

Mom gave him the royal treatment — scalp massage, a glass of chocolate milk, shampoo consultation — even though he was only seven and none of that stuff means anything to a seven-year-old. Especially a boy. But Benji isn't like other boys. He loved it and asked all sorts of questions. He wanted to smell all the products and touch all her brushes and combs. Mom was in heaven. At least until her next client showed up and she shooed him into the living room to play with me.

Benji is the kind of kid who has been teased his whole life: small, scrawny and kind of girly. He always has his nose in a magazine and hangs on the sidelines while the other boys team up for basketball. At least, he's girlier than I am, which isn't saying much since I hate dressing up and could care less about stupid teen magazines. You would think having a mother who owned a hair salon would have made me hair crazy and fashion conscious, but I told her ages ago she'd better

6

find someone else to leave the Hair Emporium to, because the minute I'm done high school I'm going to Hollywood to become an actress. I'll be famous, and all those people who made fun of me or underestimated me will be sorry they weren't nicer to me. They'll turn on their TVs at the end of the day to see me walk across the stage to accept my Oscar, while they sit on the couch in their pyjamas eating Cheezies.

Benji has already offered to be my stylist. When you're famous, it's good to have people you can trust working for you. They are less likely to sell your diaries to a tabloid or go on late-night talk shows and blab all about your love life. Benji would never do that. Plus he's pretty good at doing hair. Mom says he has the gift of gentle hands and I have to agree with her. Sometimes between clients Mom will teach him how to do a new updo or the correct way to blow someone's hair out straight. Benji practises on me and he never pulls too hard or jabs me with a bobby pin, which is more than I can say for my mother, who has been known to yank so hard that I get tears in my eyes. And she's supposed to be the professional.

Benji used to get picked on pretty bad, which is one of the reasons we became friends. He'd come home snivel-ling away and my mother would run out screaming blue murder at the boys who'd knocked him down. She'd take him by his hand and march him right into the salon, where she'd sit him down and sponge away the blood and dirt. Afterwards she'd mix up a special batch of foundation to cover the bruising. Sometimes she'd sweep a little blush on his cheeks to give him "a healthy glow." I guess she figured if it looked like Benji got out once in awhile the kids would think he was a healthy, robust kid who could handle him-self in a fight. Poor Benji went from being the wimpy kid to the weirdo kid who wore makeup. But it didn't seem to bother him much — didn't stop him from hanging around the salon, asking my mother all sorts of questions about her hair care line. Ever since then we've walked home together and somewhere along the way we became best friends.

***

Faking a phone call is a lot harder than faking a signature. With a signature you can put a piece of tissue paper over a sample of handwriting and trace it a few times until you get the hang of it. Plus, you can always do it in pencil and then trace over it in pen when you get it just right. You only have one chance for a phone call, so you have to get it right the first time. Also, you can't say "like" and "um" all the time. You have to lower your voice and know the right questions to ask.

"Okay, let's practise one more time. You be the school, I'll be the parent."

Benji sighs. "Okay."

"Ring, ring."

"Hello?"

"Benji, you have to say the name of the school."

"Right. Ferndale Public School."

I put on my best bossy Mom voice. "Yes, hello. To whom am I speaking, please?"

"Mrs. Davis, secretary."

"Good day, Mrs. Davis. I would like to speak to a Miss Ross."

"Okay."

"Benji! You didn't ask me who I was!"

"Sorry," Benji apologizes. "Who are you?"

"My name is Annie Delaney and I am a parent of a student at the school."

"Please hold, Mrs. Delaney."

"It's Miss Delaney. I'm not married."

Benji's eyes widen.

"Do you really think she'd say that? She'd correct Mrs. Davis?"

"Of course she would. Mom corrects everybody. It has to be believable."

Finally, after three practice rounds, I'm ready to give it a go. I make Benji go upstairs and find something for us to eat while I make the phone call. I can't have him distracting me while I'm in character.

The phone seems to ring for an awfully long time before there's a click and Mrs. Davis picks up.

"Ferndale Public School."

This is it! I take a deep breath and speak in my calmest voice.

"Yes, good day, I was wondering if I could speak with a Miss Ross."

"I'm sorry, the staff have left for the day."

"Oh, of course," I think quickly. "Well my name is Annie Delaney and I am just calling to, uh, confirm, that my daughter, Clarissa Louise Delaney, has indeed been placed in 7B."

"One moment, please."

Mrs. Davis puts me on hold. My heart seems to throb in time with the beeping sound the phone makes while I wait. I hold the receiver away from my mouth and take deep breaths. Benji comes down the stairs, a giant freezie in each hand.

"Well?" he whispers.

"I'm on hold," I hiss. "Don't look at me! You'll mess me up!"

Benji looks around for some place to hide.

"Where do you want me to go?" he asks.

"Thank you for holding, Mrs. Delaney—"

"It's Miss," I insist, turning my back on Benji.

"Miss Delaney," Mrs. Davis repeats. "I see here that Clarissa will be in 7B."

It's all I can do to keep from whooping and hollering, but I regain my composure and think calmly, like an adult. In my most polite voice I ask, "Might I enquire if a Benjamin Denton will also be in that class? I told his father, David Denton, that I would check for him."

There is another pause; I can just picture Mrs. Davis with her poufy bangs and clip-on earrings running a long pink fingernail down the list of names.

"Let me see, yes, Benjamin Denton will also be in 7B."

"Oh that's just, I mean, we're very excited. Thank you very much Mrs. Davis."

I hang up before she can ask me any more questions. When I turn around Benji is grinning, his lips stained blue from the freezie.

"We're in!" I shout.

Benji thrusts a freezie at me and we start jumping up and down, sucking on our freezies and laughing like maniacs. Mom sticks her head out from the salon and frowns at us.

"What's gotten into you two?" she asks. "You're awfully cheerful for two kids who are going back to school on Tuesday."

"I wish it was Tuesday tomorrow," I gush.

Mom looks at me like I've gone a little insane, and maybe I have.

"Now I know you've gone crazy," she says.

I ignore her. "This is going to be my year, I know it!" I hold up my freezie and say, "A toast!"

Benji lifts his freezie up and repeats, "A toast!"

"To Miss Ross!"

"To Miss Ross!" Benji says.

We down the rest of our freezies and collapse on the floor, suffering from too much excitement and wicked-bad brain freeze.

Beautiful

It's my favourite time of day, just after dinner but before the street lamps turn on. Outside the air still smells like barbequed hamburgers and the sound of the crickets is getting louder; you can hear them underneath all the yelling from the kids playing street hockey. There is a nip in the air that I swear wasn't there last week. Inside, Mom and I are staring at each other in the mirror of the Hair Emporium.

"Well," she says, testing the weight of my hair in her hands, "what'll it be this year? Blue highlights? Bangs? A fauxhawk?"

I roll my eyes. "Ha, ha. If I want to look like a weirdo, I know where to go."

Mom laughs. "Well if you ever feel like indulging in a little teenage rebellion you can always get a job at Curl Up & Dye. That is one sure way to get under my skin."

Curl Up & Dye is the newest salon in town. It falls under hipster salon in my mother's three categories of salon. Barbershops don't count because their clientele is mostly men. Hipster salons are full of stylists with tattoos and body piercings. They wear tight jeans or patterned tights and revealing tops, even the boys. You go to a hipster salon if you want to dye your hair purple or get a mohawk or want any kind of haircut that most people would find stupid.

Curl Up & Dye opened this summer and Mom has been grumbling about it ever since. The head stylist moved from Vancouver where she used to work on film sets, doing hair for movie stars.

"A gimmick," Mom said. "She won't last. Not when people realize how hard it is to grow out those mini bangs. Plus, if she was so hot in Vancouver, then what is she doing here?"

My mom's best friend Denise tapped the side of her nose. "Drugs," she said.

Denise thinks that drug dealing is the source of all mysterious wealth. "Clarissa," she said, "you stay clear away from drugs. I don't care how cute a boy is, never let him give you drugs; they will scramble your brains and wreck your skin. And that is more than my own mother ever told me."

Mall salons are usually part of a chain. They offer the cheapest rates and use products you can buy from infomercials on TV. The stylists wear white and too much makeup. My mom worked in a mall salon once called Kwick Kuts. "I gave perms and trimmed bangs for eight hours a day with a half-hour lunch and no break. I felt like a little cog in a big wheel."

To this day she hates giving perms because the smell of the chemicals reminds her of working at Kwick Kuts.

The last category is granola salons. In a granola salon, everyone talks in hushed voices and they play nature CDs on repeat all day long. If they offer you anything to drink, it's water or green tea. The hair products are all natural, all organic and full of essential oils. Mom does not buy into any of it.

"If I want to feel close to nature, I'll go camping," she'll say. "Oatmeal is for eating, not for scalp treatments."

Mom calls them granola salons because they go after the

granola hippie: "Or worse, the type who think they're hippies but spend hundreds of dollars at the mall to look like hippies." Just the word hippie makes Mom roll her eyes.

The Hair Emporium doesn't fit into any category. Mom caters to the small-town woman who wants a good haircut in a nice place, which is why the salon looks like a sunny kitchen, with fluffy white curtains, black-and-white checkerboard tiles on the floor, yellow walls and red reclining chairs. Every morning Mom burns a vanilla candle in the salon to make it smell homey. People are always saying that the Hair Emporium reminds them of the little salon in the movie *Steel Magnolias*. That makes my mom smile because it's one of her all-time favourite movies. After *Pretty Woman*, of course.

Mom smiles at me in the mirror, playing around with my hair, trying to find the perfect shape. I try to avert my eyes but it's hard when you're sitting in front of a huge mirror and your mother is staring you down. I don't spend a lot of time looking in the mirror if I can help it. I know I'm not ugly, but I'm not beautiful either. I am the tallest girl and the third-tallest person in my whole class. My legs are really long, but not in a good way, more in a pants-never-fit way. I'm flat as flat can be, which is fine with me, and my hair can't seem to decide if it would rather be straight or curly. Mostly I wear it in a ponytail to hide the fact that it is probably the worst hair you could possibly be stuck with.

"Don't worry, Clarissa," Mom says, reading my mind. "Right now your hair is all hopped up on hormones. It'll settle down once you get through puberty."

I hate it when she says words like puberty.

I have this idea of what I look like in my head, and every time I catch a glimpse of myself in the mirror, I'm always a little surprised at the person staring back. In my head, my nose is smaller, my cheeks are thinner and my eyes are more green than brown. It doesn't help that my mother is officially a knockout, with a heart-shaped face, dimples, big blue eyes and thick, honey-blond hair. She has an award to prove it. When she was seventeen Mom won the beauty pageant at the fair and came second in the regionals, not that she ever talks about it. Her official title was Dairy Queen, which had nothing to do with the restaurant, sadly, but was because the pageant was sponsored by the Dairy Farmers of Ontario.

Denise is the one who fills me in on all those stories. To hear her tell it, you would think it was Denise who won and not my mother. "Oh, Clarissa, she was a sight for sore eyes. Poor Janice Beal thought she could step dance her way to the podium, but no amount of dance training could get rid of that pug nose. Am I right, Annie?"

Mom demurs and won't say anything more about it. If she's disappointed that her daughter isn't beauty pageant material, she never mentions it. Just as well. I have no desire to prance around in a bathing suit or spend all that time smiling like an idiot. Still. One dimple might be nice.

"Do you want me to straighten it? Maybe add a few highlights?"

I don't like the way she's looking at my hair right now, like it's hopeless. Just because she *can* do stuff to it doesn't mean I want her to. It is my hair after all. If I want to shave it off or twist it into dreads it's none of her business. I brush her hands away from my head.

"I don't want to do anything with it," I say.

"Fine," Mom sighs. "A wash and a trim it is. Now close your eyes and I'll give you your scalp treatment."

Before they go to the sink for a shampoo, my mother

gives her customers a five-minute head-and-shoulder massage that she calls a scalp treatment. It's her specialty. Some people swear up and down that mom does the best dye job in town, but really, it's the massages that keep them coming back. People are always asking her if she took a course in massage therapy, but Mom says, "Nope, I was born with the magic touch."

She isn't kidding. First she starts with your shoulders, kneading them till they go all soft like Silly Putty. Then she works up your neck and her fingers slide behind your ears and into your hair as she massages the troubles right out of your head. When Mom is working her magic, people's jaws go all slack and hang-dog, and if they're really enjoying it, they drool a little. When she's done they open their eyes and blink like they're just waking up from the best sleep ever. Sometimes they can't talk until the cool rinse revives them a little. She's that good.

When I was younger Mom used to perfect her magic touch on my head. I'd crawl onto her lap, lean back against her and just sit there sucking my thumb, somewhere between asleep and awake, and let her massage away. That was before I was too old for such things. Now if I want a head massage I have to get my hair cut, just like everyone else.

Birds

Try as I might, I just can't seem to fall asleep. I've laid out my clothes, packed and repacked my backpack. I even made my lunch. I can't remember a time I was more excited to go back to school. Then again, the first day of school used to mean the death of summer. This year the first day of school means the first day of the rest of my life. In interviews, famous actors and actresses are always talking about the people who changed their lives. I can't explain it, but I just know that Miss Ross is that person for me.

I met Miss Ross in grade three. There was a robin's nest in one of the trees along the border of the playground, and a group of boys was trying to knock it down by throwing rocks at it.

"Hey!" I yelled. "Hey, back off! Leave them alone!"

A few of the kids scattered, but the older ones just laughed at me and kept on pitching stones, and anything else they could find, at the nest. You could just barely hear the baby birds, peeping away.

"How would you like it if I threw rocks at you?"

When no one answered, I grabbed a handful of gravel and started pitching stones in their direction. I wasn't aiming at their heads, not on purpose, but I'm not a great shot, so even though I meant to hit their backs, I missed a few times and hit them square in the neck. That didn't go over very well, but at least it got their attention.

"Hey! Who do you think you are?"

Suddenly the nest was forgotten and I was the new target. I held my arm across my face to protect my eyes as stones came whizzing by my head, too close for comfort. They had much better aim than I did. I turned on my heel and ran smack into Miss Ross, Benji hovering beside her.

"Are you okay?" he whispered.

"That's quite enough, gentlemen."

The boys skidded to a halt. She wasn't very tall, but Miss Ross had a way of making herself seem taller. She had what my mother would call a tall personality.

"I've taken the liberty of alerting the principal that you will be waiting for her outside her office."

They didn't look so tough anymore. Getting caught was bad enough, but getting caught by Miss Ross was the ultimate. One of them stuck his lip out and pointed at me.

"But she started it!" he whined.

Miss Ross held her hand up for silence.

"I will deal with Clarissa."

I looked up at her, mouth hanging open. She knew my name?

The boys walked off, grumbling to themselves. One of them shot me a dirty look. I raised my chin in the air and pretended not to see it. What did I have to be sorry for? I wasn't the baby-bird killer.

"Come with me, please."

But as I followed Miss Ross through the playground and toward her classroom, I got that sick feeling in my stomach. I may not have been aiming at the birds, but I did throw rocks at another person. Some people probably think that's worse. Maybe Miss Ross was one of those people. I didn't know much about her then. The older kids didn't pay a lot of attention to us younger students, so most of what we knew about her came from bits and pieces of conversations we had gathered in the hallways or on the playground. On the first day of school the kids who didn't get into her class spent lunch hour crying about it. She was like the Wizard of Oz and I was about to enter her Emerald City.

"Please come in, Clarissa."

Walking into Miss Ross's classroom was like walking into a rainbow. I didn't know where to look first. One whole side of the classroom was lined with red bookshelves, bursting with books. Easter-egg coloured kites were strung along the ceiling, which was painted light blue with white cloud patterns. Behind her desk Miss Ross had a real painting, the size of a bulletin board, of a tree that had birds in the branches instead of leaves. The birds were all different colours, too many to count.

Miss Ross smiled at the painting, running her fingers over the canvas. The paint was so thick it stuck out in shiny ridges. I wanted to touch it, too.

"I have always loved birds," Miss Ross said. She unwound her scarf from her neck and reached beneath her blouse to pull out a chain. On the end was a silver bird, wings outstretched, mid-flight. It matched a pair of earrings dangling from her ears, delicate silver feathers that glinted in the sunlight and looked almost real. She held out the necklace for me to look at it. I leaned forward but kept my arms at my sides. My hands were still grubby from the gravel; I didn't want to get dirt all over it.

"I made this a long time ago, at summer camp." Miss Ross smiled at the memory. "I hammered it myself," she explained, running her fingers over the dents.

"They look like scales," I said.

Miss Ross laughed, but in a friendly way. "They do!" she agreed. "People are always giving me things with birds on them, cards, mugs, you name it. I even have a book of bird poems. You know, the Haida people have totems to represent their clans. I've adopted the bird as my own personal totem."

"What kind of bird?" I asked.

"It changes," she said. "But right now, I'm fascinated by magpies. Magpies are collectors. They find bits of wool and thread, sometimes even lost jewellery, to decorate their nests. Each one is truly unique and beautiful."

I could see why Miss Ross liked magpies so much. Her classroom was like a magpie nest, full of beautiful things.

"What kind of bird am I?" I asked.

"You, Clarissa, have the soul of an eagle. A brave warrior and loyal friend."

I liked the sound of that.

"But even eagles must know when to cross the line," Miss Ross said gently.

"Am I in trouble?" I asked. Before she could answer, I rushed on, "Because I was just trying to save the birds! There were babies in the nest, and those boys were trying to knock it down. They would have died."

"Your friend Benji told me you were trying to protect them. That's very honourable. But there are other things you can do to stop something like this from happening again. Can you think of something else you could have done?"

"Told a teacher?" I guessed.

"Exactly. Let me deal with those boys. Throwing rocks at another person is just as bad as throwing them at birds."

"No, it's not!" I cried. "A bird can't throw rocks back!"

"You have a noble spirit, Clarissa. I admire that. But someone could have been seriously hurt. If you throw rocks at another person, you are just as bad as the person who throws rocks at the birds. The intent is still the same; to hurt another living thing. Do you see?"

When she put it like that it made sense. I felt ashamed.

"Do I have to go to the principal's office, too?" I asked.

Miss Ross smiled. Even her teeth were beautiful.

"I'm sure Principal Donner has her hands full. I'll tell you what, just this once I will make an exception. But I want you to promise me you won't throw rocks at another living thing again. Will you promise?"

"I promise," I said solemnly. She offered me her hand and we shook, like adults. The bracelets on her wrist clinked. I would have promised her anything.

"Well, Clarissa, it was nice to meet you."

And then she said the magic words.

"I look forward to having you in my class."

Blank Slate

It's the first day of school at last. My eyes snap open and I'm so awake I can barely remember what it feels like to be sleepy. I jump up and go about the business of dressing — looking over last night's decision and changing my mind. My blue shirt is new, but my old T-shirt with the tree and stitched leaves is cooler, more Miss Ross. She loves nature and the environment and you can't get more nature-y than a tree T-shirt. A tree-shirt. Ha. I'll have to remember to tell Benji that one.

I've decided to wear my hair curly. It doesn't curl everywhere, mostly at the back and underneath, but it's easier to goop it up and scrunch it than it is to straighten it. I swiped a bottle of super-hold gel "specially formulated for curly hair" from the Hair Emporium. It smells like jellybeans. When I pull the sides of my hair back with clips it looks almost pretty and you can't tell that the front pieces don't curl as much. I think it makes me look older.

I don't have to mention my hair at breakfast. Mom does it for me. "You have your father to thank for those curls," she says. I chew my cereal and pretend not to be interested. She doesn't often thank my father for anything. I don't know much about him, only that his name is Bill and apparently

21

his hair is curly. I've never even met him. He and my mom broke up before I was born and he moved out West to sell life insurance. She never even told him she was pregnant, which I used to think was a low down thing to do, but Denise assures me that where my father is concerned, nothing is too low down. Denise calls him Bill the Pill. People used to ask me if I missed him, but how can you miss someone you never knew? Plus, the way my mom and Denise talk about him, he doesn't sound like the type of father a kid would miss. Mom is careful not to say anything too nasty about him in front of me, but once I overheard her talking with Denise and she called him a piece of human lint. That's definitely not Dairy Queen talk.

More than once Denise has said to me, "Trust me honey, your father left the best part of himself behind here with your Mama." Then she pats my knee and winks at me so I'll get that she means me.

Unfortunately, Denise is my mother's best friend. She is taller than any other woman I know and has red hair that she gets touched up at the salon every four weeks. She has big feet and big hands and a horsey face, and she probably wouldn't win any beauty contests, but she makes up for it by wearing a lot of makeup and tight clothes. Denise doesn't have any kids of her own and so she thinks we're pretty dumb, which is why she goes out of her way to make sure I get her point.

If you ask me, she spends way too much time at our house. A few weeks ago she started turning up in the mornings before heading off to work. Now I wake up to the sound of her honking at something my mom said over coffee in the kitchen. The first time it happened it woke me up, and for a second I thought maybe a Canada goose had landed in our backyard. She's that bad. But sometimes she brings those little white powdery doughnuts. Like this morning. I stuff one in my mouth and take two more for lunch. Mom frowns.

"Isn't three doughnuts a little much?" she asks.

"One is for Benji," I lie.

"Oh, to be young and have such a metabolism," Denise sighs.

I roll my eyes, shout goodbye to anyone who is listening, then run over to pick up Benji. The first day of the rest of my life has begun!

***

"Your hair is different," Benji says. He's sitting on his porch picking invisible lint off his jeans. They're the same jeans he wore all last year, and yet they're not even a little bit too short. I had to buy all new things because somehow I got too long for everything over the summer. I'll probably be the second-tallest person in my class now.

I glare at him. "Good different or bad different?"

"Good different. You look," Benji thinks about it for a second, "pretty."

"Oh, great. So before I was not pretty."

"No, no, before you didn't care if you looked pretty; now it's like you care."

"Well, I don't care. I'm just trying something new."

Benji changes the subject.

"I thought you were wearing the blue shirt," he says.

"Changed my mind," I say, shrugging my shoulders like it's no big deal.

Benji scrutinizes my tree-shirt. "I get it. Because Miss Ross loves the environment—"

"Not *just* because of that," I protest. "I also think it's a cool shirt. You said it was a cool shirt, remember?" I feel a little embarrassed. I wonder if Miss Ross will think it's too obvious. "Besides, it's my *tree*-shirt," I finish lamely.

Benji breaks out into a smile and laughs. "A tree-shirt! That's a good one!"

I feel much better. If something is even a little bit funny, Benji will laugh out loud and he doesn't care who hears him. It doesn't matter if he's in a movie theatre, a classroom or just walking down the street. If it's funny, he laughs. He should start a business where comedians pay him to come and sit at their shows. He'd make a fortune.

"Come on, I don't want to be late!"

"We've got ages," Benji points out.

"If we stay any longer Denise will come out and go on and on about her feet."

Benji perks up a little. "Denise is over?"

I forgot that for some reason Benji is not bothered by Denise's honking laugh or the fact that she can't open her mouth without telling you too much information. I swing my backpack over my shoulder and start walking. "I'm leaving!" I call.

"I'm coming, I'm coming!"

***

"Hi, Clarissa! Hi, Benji!"

Mattie Cohen pulls herself away from a knot of people and runs in our direction. She is the only person I know who still wears a dress on the first day of school. This one is navy-blue and forest-green plaid with buttons all the way down the front. She's wearing it with a white blouse and knee socks, actual knee socks, even though it's at least twenty degrees already. She looks like she should be going to Hogwarts.

"Hi, Mattie."

"Your hair looks nice, Clarissa."

I wish I could say I liked Mattie's hair or her dress, but I don't think I can manage to say the words without smirking, and I am trying to be nicer this year.

"Thanks."

"How was your summer?"

"Fine."

"Mine was amazing! I went to camp and joined the swim team and I even babysat for my neighbours once. They had a new baby. Can you believe it? I'm not even thirteen yet and they let me babysit their brand-new baby."

Ugh. If there is anything I hate more than Mattie Cohen, it's babies.

"That's nice. Come on Benji."

"I really like your dress, Mattie."

"I said, come *on*, Benji."

Finally the bell goes and we all shuffle into the classroom. This is it, the moment I have been waiting for since that day in grade three. Maybe even before that. I'm not bad at school, but I'm not the best, either. Despite that, I have a feeling that this is the year I will amaze everyone with my artistic abilities and math skills. I, Clarissa, who have never been able to draw anything but stick people, will suddenly be making masterpieces. Miss Ross will call my mother to discuss the deep and meaningful poems I'll be writing in language arts. The choir teacher will beg me to sing the solo at the Christmas assembly. Maybe I've been a genius all along but none of the other teachers were smart enough to see it. If anyone can, it's Miss Ross.

So you can imagine my disappointment when a skinny man with red hair opens the door and says, "Goooooooood morning, ladies and gentle-monkeys. My name is Mr. Campbell and I will be your captain on the 7B ship."

Broken-hearted

Mr. Campbell tells us his first name is Tony, and then he tells us a really boring story about how people used to call him Tony the Tiger because of his name and his red hair. Worst of all, he does an impression of Tony the Tiger and doesn't even notice that only a few people are laughing at his seriously dumb joke. Benji is one of them, of course. Traitor.

"Are there any questions before we dive into science?"

I raise my hand.

"Yes, Miss—?"

"Delaney. Clarissa Delaney."

"Well, Miss Delaney, what can I do for you?"

"Where's Miss Ross?"

Tony the Tiger keeps smiling his big, dumb smile.

"I believe Miss Ross is on sabbatical," he says.

I don't know what that means, but it sounds serious and disturbingly permanent.

"Will she be coming back?"

"I'm not sure I'm the right person to ask that question of, Clarissa."

"Well, then who is?"

"I believe your question falls under the jurisdiction of personal information."

"So you don't know?"

"No, I don't know. But I *do* know we are going to have a grrrrreat year!"

I seriously doubt that.

I feel like a zombie; I sleepwalk through first period. Mr. Campbell passes out textbooks and workbooks and talks about the year ahead, but I can't concentrate. Benji keeps trying to catch my eye but I pretend not to notice. I'm so disappointed I might cry or hit something, and neither of those things are a good way to start grade seven.

All of the colour has been drained from the room. Gone is the huge painting of the tree behind the desk. Instead, Mr. Campbell has posted a big map stuck all over with pushpins. At the top the title *Where in the World Has 7B Been?* is spelled out in green and blue letters cut from construction paper. The window ledges have been cleared of all plants. Gone are the little red bookshelves bursting with Miss Ross's own personal collection of books. I'd imagined myself reading through them on the brightly striped bean-bag chairs that she'd kept at the back of the room. These have been replaced by a long table and plastic chairs. Worst of all, there are no birds anywhere. Try as I might, I can't find even the slightest trace of Miss Ross.

I don't know anything about this Mr. Campbell. Does he like whales? Does he write his own skits with parts for every student for the Christmas assembly? Does he play the guitar and hold singalongs in class? Does he know that everyone at Ferndale Public School counts down the days till grade seven, when they get to be in Miss Ross's class, and that he has gone and ruined that?

VIKKI vansickle

***

At lunchtime everyone discusses Mr. Campbell and whether or not he is married with kids. Well, not everyone. Mostly Mattie Cohen and her friends, but they're so loud it feels like the whole room is talking about it.

"He's pretty cute. Don't you think he's cute?"

"For a teacher."

"Well, I think he's cute. I bet he has a nice wife and a baby."

I could care less about stupid Mr. Campbell and his stupid wife and baby. He is not Miss Ross and that is all that counts.

***

When the world's longest school day is finally over, I practically run through the halls and out the door. Ah, freedom. I take a deep breath. It still smells like summer.

"Wait up!" Benji gets caught behind a group of grade eight boys. They move together forming a wall of solid jerk and laugh as he tries to find a way around them.

"What's the rush?" one of them jeers.

"Yeah, where's the fire?"

They push him around a bit and one of them horks loudly, aiming dangerously close to Benji's shoe. Finally he manages to squeeze through them and runs to catch up. His cheeks are pink and he's breathing pretty hard.

"Jerks," I mutter. "Come on, I need a Slurpee."

We walk in silence to the 7-Eleven. I'm afraid I might cry if I open my mouth, and Benji knows better than to bring it up, but we're both thinking the same thing. It's going to be a long year. Other kids go by, laughing and shouting, but I can't bring myself to join in. I can't stop thinking of the year I had planned, all the awards and gold stars I was going to receive.

Not even an extra-large blue raspberry Slurpee makes me feel any better. I gulp down as much as I can before the brain freeze kicks in and I have to stop because it hurts too much.

"Nerds?" Benji offers.

I put out my hand and he taps the box: a pile of neon green candy falls into my palm. I dump it into my Slurpee and watch as the neon green stains the Slurpee a dark, muddy colour.

"Gross," Benji says.

"It looks almost as bad as I feel," I say.

We keep walking in silence until Benji says, "If we hurry we can still watch *Full House*." I snort. Like that will make me feel better.

Benji's all-time favourite TV show is this old series he discovered in reruns called *Full House*. He loves the idea of all those people living together. Not me. I'd go crazy with all those uncles and sisters around. Especially that Michelle Tanner. She is my least favourite character. People are always forgiving her because she's so cute. If you ask me, that Michelle Tanner knows she is cute and uses it to get away with things. They show a full hour of *Full House* at four o'clock. I would rather watch one of those real-life rescue shows, but Benji says they give him nightmares and my mother says the sound of all the sirens and screaming upsets her clients. So, I lose. At least Uncle Jesse is pretty funny.

***

"We're home!"

Mom says something back, but I can tell she's with a client. Benji and I drop our backpacks in the kitchen, grab some cookies and head down to the basement. Down the stairs and immediately to the left is the Hair Emporium. Straight ahead is the den. Mom usually schedules ten minutes between clients, so there's rarely a time when someone has to wait, but just in case, she lugged two of our dining room chairs downstairs to create a waiting area outside the salon. Between the chairs is a coffee table stacked high with magazines; most of them are hair magazines, but we also get subscriptions to *People* and *Hello! Canada* so clients can check out the celebrity hairstyles, too. One of my jobs is to make sure the new magazines are put out every week.

"No one wants to go to a hair salon and read last year's magazines," Mom says. "They'll think we're out of date."

When I was little I used to like hanging out in the waiting room and chatting with Mom's clients. But now I'd rather be left alone with Benji and the TV. Last year Mom put up three Japanese dressing screens to divide the waiting area from the rest of the den. Even with the screens, when Mom has a client I have to keep the TV on low, which is sort of unfair, since it's my house, too. But Mom says that television doesn't set the right sort of atmosphere for a salon. Instead, she has a radio tuned to the country station. She says country songs are full of people pouring their hearts out, "just like hair salons. People come in for a cut and colour, but they also come in to chat about what's bothering them. So when they leave, their heads and their hearts are just a little bit lighter."

Benji and I stare at the TV, but he's the only one watching. I keep imagining the year as it should have been, and I start feeling worse and worse. I'm impatient for Benji and Mom's clients to leave so I can have her all to myself, just for a little while.

***

At the end of the day Mom walks her last client up the stairs, says goodbye at the door and then comes back down to the salon and cranks up the radio. This is my signal to grab the cleaning bucket from under the kitchen sink and make my way to the salon for Power Hour.

The name Power Hour comes from a churchy TV show that's on Sunday mornings; it's for people who can't make it out to real church. In our house, Power Hour is an hour of intense cleaning, so named because of two things. One, my mother is a furious cleaner who likes to get the job done fast, and two, she is a firm believer in the saying, "Cleanliness is next to godliness." Even though the joke is a little bit lame, in a mom-joke kind of way, I love Power Hour.

One of the few things I have inherited from my mother is a love of cleaning. I hate mess of any kind and one of my favourite smells is my Mom's homemade cleaning solution, which Denise calls Annie-Off. Annie-Off smells like lemons and vinegar and something else I can't put my finger on. It's kind of sharp and spicy, like something you might smell in an Indian restaurant. You can use Annie-Off on any surface and it never leaves a residue or feels greasy. Plus, it's made of all-natural ingredients, which is better for the environment. The recipe for Annie-Off is top secret, and if there's one thing my mom is better at than cleaning, it's keeping a secret. She mixes up a big batch once a month while I'm at school, and I come home to find a row of spray bottles from the dollar store lined up under the kitchen sink. It's maddening. I have suggested many times that we sell Annie-Off and make tons of money, but Mom says some things she'd rather keep in the family. Fine for her, but when she dies and leaves me the recipe, I am going to sell Annie-Off and make a million dollars.

During Power Hour Mom looks after the individual stations, the sink, the dryers and all the combs and brushes. My job is to sweep and mop the floors, clean the mirrors and change the garbage. I also vacuum the waiting area, primp the magazines and dust the figurines. We make a good team, Mom and I. It normally takes us less than an hour, except for the times Denise stops by, plops herself down in one of the swirly chairs, kicks her shoes off and yells over the music while we clean. She never offers to pick up a broom or help disinfect the combs and scissors. It's like she doesn't notice we're in the middle of something. Typical Denise.

I am just starting to feel a bit better, all that cleaning clearing my head, when I hear the back door slam and Denise is clomping down the stairs, already yammering on about some "idiot" at the Shoppers Drug Mart in Leasdale who "wouldn't know a lipstick from a crayon."

Mom listens and nods and makes supportive noises.

"*Mmm, hmm* . . . He didn't! Oh, poor DeeDee."

Poor DeeDee? So she spent a few bad hours with a real jerk. After today she'll never have to deal with him, whereas I am stuck with Tony the Tiger for an entire school year. I wait for a break in Denise's tirade but there doesn't appear to be one. I can't get a word in edgewise.

Since no one seems to care about my day, I am sure to make as much noise as possible in my cleaning, sighing occasionally, until finally Denise picks upon it.

"What's gotten into you?" she asks.

"Well, school was terrible, thanks for asking," I say.

"It's just the first day," Mom says. "I'm sure things will get better."

That's it? "It's just the first day?" "I'm sure things will get better?" I wait for the supportive noises and the "Poor Clarissa," but they don't come. Unbelievable.

"You shouldn't frown like that, it'll give you wrinkles," Denise says, "and then you'll really have something to frown about." She tries to run her fingers through my hair but I am too fast for her.

"You were such a cutie pie when you were a kid. Blond as blond can be. Perfect little curls. The longest god-given eyelashes I ever saw. Your mom could have put you in commercials."

"Now Denise, you know how I feel about mothers who push their kids into the business," Mom says.

Denise sighs and for once I agree with her. What is so bad about being on TV?

"Not even one Little Miss competition," Denise says. "And you with your mother's genes. It's a crying shame."

Mom catches my eye in the mirror and winks. "Clarissa here would have thrown a fit and you know it," she says.

"Well, that time has passed," she says, giving me the once over and frowning. "At least you've still got those long lashes."

What I would like to do is kick Denise as hard as I can. Instead, I happen to "trip" while emptying the dust pan into the garbage, and a pile of hair clippings lands all over her feet. Denise jumps up, shaking her legs.

"Lord Almighty, you should be more careful, Clarissa!"

"Sorry, Denise. I guess I had trouble seeing through my long lashes."

Before she can respond I dash out of the salon and run up the stairs two at a time, locking myself in my bedroom. Even from there, beneath the sounds of Denise ranting about what a horrible child I am, I can hear my mother laughing.

Basketball

I don't see the ball coming. One second I'm walking out of the school, and the next I'm on my hands and knees on the pavement and there are yellow spots dancing in front of my eyes. I hear yelling, and my name, and then someone is kneeling beside me.

"Are you okay, Clarissa?"

The yellow spots are quickly being replaced by tears. I blink to keep them back and grit my teeth to stop myself from whimpering like a baby. My head is throbbing where the ball smacked it and my hands hurt. When I hold them up for inspection they're pink and scraped. I rub them gently against my T-shirt to get rid of the gravelly pieces.

"We didn't see you, I swear. Are you okay? Do you want me to get a teacher?"

Michael Greenblat is holding a dirty basketball under one arm and looking guilty. As he should.

"You should be more careful!" I manage to shout. "I could have a concussion!"

Michael's ears turn pink and he looks like he might cry, although he isn't the one who was viciously attacked by a bunch of moronic basketball players.

"I'm sorry, I really am. We were just tossing it around and then all of a sudden you were in the way. I mean, you weren't in the way, but you weren't there, and then you were and so was the ball . . ." Michael trails off lamely and I glare at him, pressing my hand against my forehead to try and stop the throbbing. It doesn't seem to be working. In fact I think it's getting worse.

"Do you want me to walk you home?"

"No, I'm waiting for Benji."

"I'm really, really sorry."

I sniff and wait for him to slink back to his dumb basketball-playing friends, who keep calling after him, but Michael just stands there, staring at me. Where is Benji? I don't know how much longer I can stand here without crying and I refuse to let Michael Greenblat see me cry. My head is really starting to hurt. I think I can feel a goose-egg swelling under my hands.

Wonderful.

Finally, Benji appears.

"What happened?" he asks.

"They hit me with their stupid basketball," I explain.

"By accident!" Michael insists. "It was an accident."

"I think I have a concussion," I continue.

I don't know who looks more worried, Benji or Michael.

"You should put ice on it," Michael says.

"If it wasn't for you, I wouldn't have to put ice on anything," I say. "Come on, Benji, let's go. See you tomorrow, Michael."

I turn to leave but look back over my shoulder and add, "If I'm not in a coma, that is."

***

Benji knows not to pester me about my head injury. I have to keep sniffing to stop myself from crying. When we get home, Mom doesn't even acknowledge us. She's too busy with a client.

Benji roots around in the freezer until he finds a package of frozen peas for me to hold against my head, while I go search for the children's Tylenol, the chewable kind that tastes like grape Sweetarts. I think about telling Mom what happened but decide not to. She can't even take two seconds to ask me about school. I'll probably end up in the hospital with massive brain trauma. Serves her right for not caring enough to ask me how my day was.

We slink down the stairs and crash in front of the TV, homework spread out in front of us. It's only the second day of school and already we have lists of projects and assignments. As if my head didn't hurt enough. Benji flips half-heartedly through the channels.

"What do you want to watch?" he asks.

"Put in the Wizard," I say.

My all-time favourite movie is *The Wizard of Oz*. I could watch that movie every day for the rest of my life and never get sick of it. I even tried to once when I was little. I would come home from daycare, put the tape in and settle down inches from the TV. Mom would holler at me to move back before I went cross-eyed, but I couldn't move. I was too mesmerized. Finally she'd hook her hands under my armpits and yank me back until I was a safe distance away from the screen, muttering about lazy eyes and glasses.

Benji's favourite part of the movie was when Glinda came down in the pink bubble.

"How do you think they did that?" he'd ask.

"*Shhh*," I'd say.

We used to play Oz, pretending that the mat at the bottom of the stairs was the Deadly Desert — like in the books, which were way more exciting than the movie. You had to jump over the mat to get to safety. I was always Dorothy and used one of mom's beaded belts as Dorothy's magic belt. Benji would be all sorts of different characters, but his favourite was Glinda the Good, even though she was a girl.

We haven't played Oz in a long time. It's not the same anymore. We're getting too old for that kind of make believe. Instead, we plop ourselves down in front of the TV and eat as many cookies as we can before six o'clock, when Mr. Denton bangs on the screen door and hollers down the stairs for Benjamin. The sound of his big fist rattling the window panes makes me jump right out of my skin every time. And it's not just me overreacting, because under her breath, I hear my mother swear, "Jesus H. Christ."

Now Benji is the kind of kid who has the sad look down pat, but I never see him look sadder than when his dad comes banging on the back door. He dunks his Oreo one last time before practically swallowing it whole.

"Cripes, Benji. Doesn't your dad feed you?"

He takes his own sweet time getting up, sweeping the crumbs off the table, putting his glass on the counter and saying his goodbyes to Mom.

"Thank you, Miss Delaney."

"Call me Annie, sweetheart."

"Thank you, Miss Annie."

"Close enough. You're welcome, Benji. We'll see you tomorrow."

"Yes, Miss Annie. Well, goodbye again. Bye, Clarissa."

Then he creeps up the stairs in that annoying way he has,

where he can't move onto the next step until both feet are on the stair before. It's amazing he gets anywhere on time.

"Poor little thing. You be nice to him, Clarissa."

"I am nice to him!"

"Not everyone is as lucky as you."

Lucky? Who said anything about lucky?

***

Denise arrives just after six to get her roots done. So much for Power Hour. She sits with her feet up on the counter, drinking coffee and eating her way through a pack of powdered doughnuts.

"You wouldn't believe the day I had," Denise says. "I'm on my third coffee and I'm not sure if I'll make it to eight o'clock."

"What's at eight o'clock?" I ask.

"Dinner with the Monster."

The Monster is Denise's sister Linda. Every few months they get together to brag about their lives. Linda is a travel agent with two kids, a dog and a husband. Denise calls her the Monster, but she sounds more boring than monstrous to me. Then again, she is related to Denise, so there must be something wrong with her.

"How was your day, baby?" Mom asks. Finally.

"Awful. I got hit in the head with a basketball."

"Let me see." Mom pushes back my hair and squints at my forehead. "It can't be too serious. I don't see anything."

"Well it hurts!" I say.

"I'm sure it does, but it'll feel better tomorrow."

Ugh. It's like she doesn't even *care*.

"And Mr. Campbell is trying to ruin grade seven for me."

"Not *Tony* Campbell," says Denise. "I met him last week

at the grocery store. He's a real cutie, if you like red hair."

"You have red hair," I point out.

"Thanks to your mama," Denise winks and pops another doughnut into her mouth. The powdered sugar sticks to her lipstick. "He seemed like a decent guy to me."

"Well, he's not, and he's married, anyway," I say savagely.

Denise shrugs. "Want a doughnut?" she asks.

"No," I sigh, eyeing their mugs. "What I really could use is a coffee."

Mom shakes her head and holds her coffee cup close to her chest.

"Nuh-uh. Coffee stunts your growth and ruins your teeth."

"You drink it."

"I have no choice; I'm addicted."

"Denise drinks it."

"Denise is an adult. She can choose to ruin her teeth if she wants to."

"That's not fair."

"Life's not fair, baby. But at least you'll have good teeth."

She reaches out to straighten a curl, but I duck away before she can get her powdery fingers in my hair.

"Mom, gross. There's sugar all over your fingers."

She looks down at them and licks the sugar off, one finger at a time.

"So there is. What would I do without you?"

Since it is clear to me that no one in this room cares about my day or how I'm going to survive an entire year with Tony the Tiger, I stomp up the stairs and leave them to their coffee and their highlighting.

The Blues

In addition to being next-door neighbours, Benji and I are right next to each other on the class list because Denton comes right after Delaney in roll call. This means that every time we are split up alphabetically, which is a lot, we are put in the same group. It also means we end up sitting near each other in class. But not this year, the year of Mr. Campbell. He thinks it would be fun to "mix it up." Every week he arranges us by something different: birth date, height, even zodiac sign. I told him I don't go in for all that zodiac hocus-pocus.

"Astrology has a fascinating history, Clarissa. Whether or not you believe in it, people have done some very interesting things based upon their star sign."

"Like seating arrangements?" I ask.

"Among other things, yes."

"Well, it seems like a load of you-know-what, if you'll excuse my language."

"What is it about astrology that bothers you, Clarissa?"

"Well, it's a lot like stereotyping, and we learned last year in Mrs. Miller's class that it is wrong to judge individual people based on group assumptions. That is how things like racism and sexism get started. Are you telling us to be prejudiced, Mr. Campbell?"

"No, I am telling you where to sit."

"Fine. But I want you to know that I think basing a seating arrangement on zodiac signs is inappropriate."

"Spoken like a true Aries. Now please take your seat."

***

More proof that Mr. Campbell is the worst thing to happen to Ferndale Public School: his idea of a school project is a radio station. Just before lunch he announces that he's starting a radio club for anyone who's interested in helping out. Poor Mr. Campbell. Doesn't he know that no one listens to the radio anymore? I almost feel sorry for him.

"We'll have two programs," he explains. "A daily lunchtime program with music, school news and interest stories, and a ten minute special we'll do once a month on a topic of our choice."

Hands go up and Mr. Campbell answers all sorts of questions. Yes, the club will be open to the whole school; yes, there could be an all-request lunch hour; yes, they could interview outside people. Mr. Campbell is so excited about his club he forgets to assign us math homework. I guess there is a silver lining in every cloud.

***

We're almost out the door when Mattie calls after us.

"Hi, Benji! Hi, Clarissa! Are you going to join the radio club?"

I snort. "No way."

Benji shrugs. "I don't like public speaking," he says.

"It's not like that at all, silly. You talk into a microphone in a room with no audience," Mattie says brightly.

Benji is not convinced. "Still—"

41

"Well, I am," Mattie breezes on. "I think it's a great idea. I don't know if you remember, but I did morning announcements last year."

I roll my eyes. "We remember."

"So, I already have experience."

"Sounds good."

"Can I walk with you?"

Benji and I exchange glances.

"If you want to," I say.

"Great! So what do you think about having a Guess That Song contest?"

Mattie talks about contests and giveaways all the way to the corner of Blair Avenue and Chestnut Street. Benji suggests getting gift certificates from local businesses.

"That's a great idea!" Mattie says. "Are you sure you don't want to join the radio club?"

"Well, maybe behind-the-scenes stuff," he says.

"Do you think your mom might donate a gift certificate for the salon?" Mattie asks me.

I shrug. "Maybe. Well, this is where we turn," I say.

Mattie stops.

"Oh," she says. Something about the way she stands there fiddling with her skirt makes me think she's waiting for me to ask her over, but that doesn't make any sense. Mattie has lots of friends who are much more interested in things like clothes and the radio club than I am. Maybe she just has to go to the bathroom.

"So, see you tomorrow?"

"Okay! Don't forget to bring your newspaper article for current events!"

"I won't."

"And ask your mom about the gift certificate!"

"I'll think about it. Bye, Mattie."

"Bye, Clarissa! Bye Benji!"

We watch her turn and go.

"Is she skipping?" I ask.

"No, she's just a bouncy walker," Benji says.

Cripes.

***

"We ordered pizza," Mom says. I don't feel like talking. I grunt instead.

"Pardon me?"

I grunt a little bit louder.

"We don't speak caveman," Mom says sweetly. Denise slaps her thigh and explodes into her big honking laugh.

Anger crackles underneath my skin. I swear, if someone touched me right now they'd get such a big electrical shock they'd probably fall down dead.

"Not hungry," I say shortly.

Mom reaches out and grabs my wrist as I squeeze by.

"Where are you going? Tell us about your day," she says with her you-can-talk-to-me-I'm-a-good-mother smile. It makes me even angrier.

I yank my arm back.

"I don't want to."

Mom sighs dramatically. "I can't wait till we're through the angsty period."

She's talking to Denise, but she makes sure to say it loud enough so that I can hear. When I get to my room, I am sure to slam the door hard enough to make the pictures on the wall in the living room rattle.

***

A little bit later there is a knock at the door. I consider pretending to be asleep, but I can smell the pizza from here and it's making my stomach growl.

"Clarissa? The pizza is here."

My hunger melts away any bit of resolve I had left. When I open the door Mom is standing there with the pizza and an armful of movies and I forget to be mad at her.

"I thought maybe you needed some Julia Roberts," she says.

Mom has seen every Julia Roberts movie about seven hundred times. Her favourites are *Steel Magnolias*, because it's about a hair salon, and *Pretty Woman*, because every stylist loves a makeover story. She knows all the words to both and gets choked up at the same parts every time. It's one thing for Benji and me to obsess over movies, but my mother is a grown woman. After a particularly bad day she'll say, "That was a Julia Roberts kind of day," and then I know we're in for popcorn and manis and pedis. My job is to pop two bags of microwave popcorn while my mother sets up a mini nail salon.

She clears the TV guides and junk mail off the coffee table and lays out what Denise refers to as Annie's Arsenal. All Mary Kay, all supplied by Denise. My mom keeps her nail supplies in a plastic case under the bathroom sink. It's full of Q-tips, cotton swabs and all kinds of nail polish. There are emery boards, cuticle pushers, nail clippers and even a buffer pad. The emery boards look like Popsicle sticks covered in pink sandpaper. Usually I get to pick my nail polish, but tonight Denise has all sorts of opinions.

"Nothing too pink, Clarissa, that's a summer shade. And nothing too red, it'll stain your nails."

My favourite colour is called Ocean Pearl, and it goes on light pink with white swirls in it. It makes my fingernails look like the insides of tiny seashells.

Usually it's just me, Mom and Julia Roberts, but tonight Denise is overstaying her welcome.

"I just love that Richard Gere," she says. "How come I can't find a man like that around here? You know they say he's a Buddhist."

"*Mmmm.*" Mom paints my nails one stroke at a time. I love the way the polish feels on my nails, cool and silky. It takes almost the whole movie to finish. First you have to put on a base coat, let it dry for ten minutes, then follow up with two thin coats of colour. After that sits, you finish with a top coat, which takes at least ten minutes to dry. The bottle says quick-dry, but Denise says you never can trust a label. She would know; she sells the stuff. We start with our toes and finish with our fingernails.

"Aren't we a sight? All spiffed up and nowhere to go."

I want to tell Denise that she is welcome to leave anytime, but my beautiful nails are putting me in such a good mood that I don't bother.

Bully

"Hey, where are you goin'?"

Terry DiCarlo steps out from his group of low-life grade eight thugs and stands between Benji and the door to the boy's bathroom. His friends laugh like they've never heard anything funnier in their lives and turn to watch, arms crossed, tough guy looks on all their faces.

"I'm just going to the bathroom," Benji mutters, keeping his head down.

"You're going the wrong way," Terry says, and he grabs Benji's shoulder and slams him into the girls' bathroom so hard that Benji falls through the door and into the bathroom. Inside, someone who sounds a lot like Mattie Cohen shrieks, "*Benji!* This is the *girls'* bathroom!"

Benji stumbles back out, rubbing his elbow, which is almost as red as his face. He keeps his back to the wall and inches away from Terry, like a dog who knows it's about to be kicked. Anger fills me up and before I can stop myself, words are coming out of my mouth.

"I guess it's true," I say, nice and loud, so everyone who wasn't already watching turns to look at us.

Terry narrows his mean eyes. "What? That your little

boyfriend would rather do your hair than take you out on a date like a real man?"

"No, it must be true that they're keeping you back a year because you're too dumb to read. Only an idiot can't tell the difference between the words 'girl' and 'boy.'"

"You think you're funny? You little—"

But I don't hear the rest of what he says. I'm too busy walking away. Behind me some people are laughing and others are egging Terry on, but I hold my head high and march over to my locker. He can't hurt me, I'm a girl. Plus, I don't care what Terry DiCarlo thinks.

When I get to my locker my hands are shaking so badly I can't make the dial move where I want it to go. I feel angry and nervous and exhilarated, like I could take on a whole room full of Terrys or jump off a ten-storey building and land on my feet. Suddenly Benji is beside me, taking the lock from my jittery hands.

"Here, I'll do it," he says. His voice is wobbly, like it's full of tears.

"That Terry DiCarlo makes me so mad," I say. "What a jerk."

Benji nods and pulls off the lock. I grab my books and coat and pretend to be busy shoving them into my backpack so he can wipe his eyes, which have started to get teary. Then I slam the door and we boot it out of there, as fast as we can without running. School is the last place you want to be when you're upset because nothing is ever private. There's always someone staring at you, ready to run off and tell everyone that you picked your nose at lunch or were crying at your locker.

***

Benji is even quieter than usual on the way home. I do impressions of Amanda and Min's oral presentation on some ridiculous book about horses, complete with hair-chewing (Amanda) and baby-talk (Min), but his cheek doesn't even twitch. I buy him the king-size Mars bar at the 7-Eleven but he just stashes it in his backpack. Normally he'd have it polished off before we got home.

Even Mom, Benji's favourite person in the whole world, can't seem to wipe the gloom off his face. When she pops her head around the screen and asks how our days were, he just shrugs. Mom's eyebrows go up and she looks at me as if maybe I did something. I shrug. I don't want to embarrass Benji any more by going into the details.

"Did someone's dog die?" she asks.

No one says anything. She runs a hand through Benji's hair, rubbing the ends between her fingers.

"You need a trim, Benji," she says. "I've got fifteen minutes before Tracey arrives and she's always late anyways."

Benji gets up wordlessly and follows her into the Hair Emporium like a sad puppy. After five minutes she has massaged the words out of his head and Benji is blubbering about Terry. Mom is all honey and sweetness and understanding, but later, after he's left and Power Hour has begun, she cleans like a maniac, shining the stations so hard I worry that she'll take all the gloss right off.

"How long has this thing with Terry been going on?" she asks.

"I don't know, awhile, I guess."

The truth is Benji has always been the butt of people's jokes, but after awhile people just got used to him and left him alone. This thing with Terry was new. Terry was so much bigger and meaner.

"Does your teacher know?"

I roll my eyes. "No, he's too dumb to pick up on it. He'd probably just lock them in a room together and make them talk it out anyway."

Mom frowns. "I still think he should know," she says. "What about David?"

I snort. "Yeah, right. He'd just tell him to fight back."

Benji's dad was something of a hockey star in high school, always getting into fights, which is how he got his nickname, the Dentonator.

According to Mom, "Just about the only thing David Denton was good at was hockey, but he got himself a bum knee just out of high school. No NHL for him. It's too bad, because he could have been great."

Benji never says much about it. He's heard the stories from his dad a million times, and he's seen the trophy case and the newspaper cuttings. Front and centre on the Dentons' fridge is the newspaper article from when his dad's hockey team won the junior championships almost fifteen years ago. It's so old the paper is discoloured, like milk gone sour.

Any idiot could see that Benji was not going to follow in his father's footsteps. My mother calls him "a delicate child." He's short for his age, scrawny, with little wrists, bony shoulders and skin so pale you can see the blue veins underneath. Not exactly hockey material.

Benji doesn't even like to watch hockey, let alone play it. One year the Dentonator signed him up for peewee hockey, hoping to toughen him up. He only lasted one year, most of which he spent on the bench watching the other boys slamming into the boards, the net and each other. After a practice or a game he'd come over to our house bruised and crying because his toes were so cold they hurt. Mom would make us hot chocolate while Benji sat huddled on the floor with his feet on the air vents, defrosting. If it was really bad, she'd crank the heat up and drape a blanket over his knees so the hot air came rushing on and puffed out the blanket like a hot-air balloon.

At the end of the season, the coach told the Dentonator that Benji just didn't have what it takes to be a hockey player. Boy was he mad. He called the coach all sorts of names and raged about finding a better team with a better coach. But in the end he never bothered. Even Benji's thick-headed, hockey-crazed father had to admit that his son was never going to play in the NHL. And so Benji's hockey career came to an end.

"As thick as he may be, I still think David should know about Terry," Mom says. "And your teacher, too."

Oh, right. I know exactly what the school will do. They'll make Terry and Benji sit down with a mediator and talk it out. Then after school Terry will hunt Benji down and cream him anyway. I pretend not to hear her over the hum of the DustBuster.

"Clarissa! I'm talking to you."

Mom stops rubbing the finish off the countertops and stares at me, hands on her hips, cheeks rosy from her mani-acal scrubbing. Figures — my cheeks get all splotchy and shiny when I'm working hard, but she still looks beautiful.

"I heard you," I mutter.

"Do you want to do it, or shall I give them both a call?"

"I will," I say quickly.

"Good."

Mom is cleaning at a much calmer pace. I breathe a sigh of relief and go back to my DustBusting. That was a close one. I have no intention of telling the Dentonator or Mr. Campbell about Terry DiCarlo, at least not yet. It would just make things worse. I know she thinks she's doing the right thing, but she has no idea what goes on at school. How can she? She was the Dairy Queen! She probably just smiled at anyone who was giving her a hard time and they melted on the spot and offered to carry her books for her. She has no idea what school is like for regular people. Life must be so much easier when you're beautiful.

Boys

Later that night the doorbell rings and my mother yells, "Clarissa, there's a young man at the door for you."

I assume she means Benji, until I walk through the kitchen and see her and Denise smirking behind magazines.

"What?" I say.

They just shake their heads and glance at each other over the tops of *Cosmo*. It makes me so mad that when I open the door, I practically shout, "What is it?" only to find Michael Greenblat staring at me. He steps back a little and I feel bad about yelling at him.

"Oh, hi," I say, in a much more normal tone of voice.

Michael's face relaxes into a smile. "Hi, Clarissa, how are you?"

"I'm fine."

"That's good, that's good."

Then we stare at each other for a few seconds, Michael just smiling away and me wondering what he came for and whether or not I'm supposed to ask him in, even though I don't really want to.

"Are you having a good night?" he asks finally.

"I guess."

"Me too."

We look down at our feet and I'm just about to tell him I have to go, when he says, "I wanted to give you something," and pulls a rock out of his coat pocket.

"A rock?" I ask.

Michael looks offended. "It's not just a rock, it's a geode," he says. "I found it this summer at the cottage. Actually, I found a whole bunch of them at this old cave. But this is the best one. They're pretty rare."

He puts the geode in my hands. It's warm from his pocket and looks like an egg cut in half. The outside is pretty boring, just a regular old rock, grey and bumpy, but the inside is full of tiny little crystals that are just a little bit pink, like strawberry lemonade.

"That's all quartz on the inside," Michael explains.

"Are you sure you don't want to keep it?" I ask. "I wouldn't know what to do with it."

"You don't do anything. You just look at it," he says.

"Oh."

"Besides, I want you to have it."

I don't know what else to say, and apparently neither does Michael, because he scuffs the toe of his shoe against the doorframe and doesn't say a word. We don't talk much in school unless it's for a project or something. I start to get the feeling that if I don't say something soon, he might stay there all night.

"Well, thanks."

Michael brightens a little. "You're welcome."

"I'll see you tomorrow."

"Okay. Bye, Clarissa."

I barely close the door before Denise is beside me.

"Was that your boyfriend?" she asks.

Ugh. "For your information, I don't have a boyfriend."

"Well, who was it?" she insists.

"It's none of your business," I snap.

"What did he give you?" Mom asks.

"He says it's a geode."

"A geode?"

Mom takes the geode and turns it over in her hands.

"It's pretty," she says, passing it to Denise.

"Looks like a rock to me. But not the good kind." Denise wiggles her fingers and cackles at her own joke. She doesn't seem to notice that she's the only one laughing.

"Oh, that poor boy," my mother says. "I hope you were nice to him."

"I *was* nice to him!"

Denise laughs. "Oh, Clarissa, you're a real heartbreaker, just like your mama."

"You should have invited him in," Mom says.

"There's always next time," Denise adds.

Right. Like I would ever submit anyone to that kind of torture.

"If you don't mind, I have homework to do," I remind them.

"Don't forget your geode," Mom says, grinning.

I snatch it away from her and stomp off to my room, slamming the door shut behind me. I don't know why I'm embarrassed — it's Michael who should be embarrassed. Who does he think he is, giving me geodes? I consider giving it back to him tomorrow, but I don't want to hurt his feelings. Besides, it is kind of pretty. I hide it at the back of my sock drawer where no one will see it and ask questions.

When the phone rings, I'm not surprised to hear Benji's voice on the other end.

"Was that Michael Greenblat?" he asks.

"Don't you have anything better to do than spy on people from your window?"

"What did he want?"

"He gave me a geode."

"Wow. He must really like you."

"He does not."

"Remember his summer writing assignment? All he could talk about was his rock collection and going to visit real stalactites and stalagmites. He wants to be a geologist."

I snort.

"A geologist?"

"It's a person who studies rocks."

"I *know* what a geologist is, Benji. I just think it's a stupid thing to be."

"Well, Michael doesn't, and he must really like you if he gave you one of his geodes. What are you going to do?"

"I'm not going to do anything except hang up and pretend this conversation never happened."

"I think he's nice."

"Good *night*, Benji."

"Good night, Clarissa."

Brainstorming

"What do the following people have in common?"

Mr. Campbell leans over the overhead projector and scribbles three names in big, sloppy red letters: Clark Kent, Peter Parker and Bruce Wayne. Every hand of every boy in the classroom shoots up. I continue to X out the eyes of the people in my history book.

"Clarissa?"

Figures. Mr. Campbell only calls on me when my hand is not up.

"They're not real."

"Yes, that's true: these are all fictional characters. Anything else?"

"They're all boys."

"Yes, that is very observant. They are all men. Anything else? Michael?"

"They're all superheroes."

Mr. Campbell grins and high-fives Michael like he is some sort of genius. Mr. Campbell doesn't seem to notice that he has red overhead marker smeared all over the side of his arm. "Exactamundo!"

I swivel in my chair to roll my eyes at Benji, who, thanks

to this week's back-to-basics seating arrangement, is sitting behind me.

Benji leans forward and whispers, "Your ears are going red."

I whip around and shush him. "They are *not!*" But even as the words come out of my mouth, I feel my ears getting warm. Ever since Michael came over to my house to give me that stupid geode I've been watching him and thinking about him. Not a lot, but more than I used to, which was never.

Michael has floppy hair that my mother would call sandy blond and a mole on the back of his neck that is sometimes hidden by the collar of his shirt. His favourite sport is baseball and he has at least six different Blue Jays T-shirts. I don't *not* like sports; there are just a million other things I'd rather be doing. But I could learn to like baseball. Maybe Michael will be the youngest Blue Jays player ever. I could go to every game and sit in the stands and cheer him on. Then one day, after he'd hit the winning homerun in the World Series, I'd run out onto the field and jump into his arms. And Michael would get down on one knee in front of the entire stadium, the TV crews and practically the whole wide world, and propose to me, Clarissa Louise Delaney. I like that dream a lot. Maybe more than I actually like Michael.

"Now what's the difference between a hero and a super-hero?" Mr. Campbell asks.

"Easy," Michael says. "A superhero has a superpower, like superhuman strength, or controlling the weather and stuff."

"You're absolutely right, Michael. A superhero is aided by something beyond the normal capabilities of human beings. As Clarissa said, they don't exist, they're not real."

A few people actually groan, like this is surprising news.

Like maybe superheroes were just in hiding all this time. Cripes. Some people are so slow.

"Now *heroes* are everyday people, like you and me, who have done something extraordinary without the help of a superpower. Who can give me an example of heroism?"

People shout out their examples and Mr. Campbell scrambles to write them all down, smearing his arm with more red marker.

"Going to war."

"Saving someone's life."

"Firefighters!"

"Starting up a charity!"

Thankfully, the bell rings.

"Time's up folks!" Mr. Campbell caps his marker and makes a big show of wiping his forehead with the back of his hand, like he's exhausted by all that writing. "Phew! What a list! Great job, everyone. I think all of these suggestions are really terrific. But I want to hear from each of you individually. For your independent project, I want each and every one of you to write a two-page essay about a modern-day hero, someone living today who adds something to our definition of heroism. It could be anyone at all. Think outside the box."

Finally, home time. The only box I'm thinking outside of right now is the Oreo cookie box.

Boots

Somehow Terry DiCarlo has figured out how to break into Benji's locker. He doesn't seem smart enough to pick a lock, so maybe someone did it for him. When people are afraid of you, you can make them do pretty much anything.

The first time he stole all of Benji's stuff and left it in the mud outside by the track: backpack, gym clothes, textbooks, everything. Most of it we just threw in the washing machine, but cleaning the textbooks was a real pain. We had to wipe the pages, blow them dry with the hair dryer and then pile them under encyclopedias to try and flatten them because the pages had dried all puffy and wavy. They're still readable, but I bet the school will make him pay for them at the end of the year.

Now Benji carries his books with him from class to class, but he has to keep his coat and hat in his locker. Last week we found them in the lost and found. And then today, at lunch, we find Terry wearing them, dancing around pretending to be Benji, singing rude songs in a high voice that sounds nothing at all like the real Benji.

"What are you looking at?" he snarls.

"Nothing much," I say, tossing my hair and shrugging.

Terry glares at us and then spits, barely missing Benji's toe. Disgusting.

"Clarissa, let's go," Benji whispers. He's tucked his head as far down into the neck of his sweater as possible, like a turtle, and pulled the sleeves down over his hands, which are red from the cold.

"Do you want to die of hypothermia?" I ask him.

"No."

"Do you want to go home and tell your dad he needs to buy you a new coat?"

Benji shakes his head. "Definitely, no."

"Well then."

"But—"

"But, nothing. I have a plan."

I lean over and whisper in Benji's ear. "Start laughing," I hiss.

Benji looks stricken.

"What? Why?"

"Just do it."

Miracle of miracles, Benji manages to force a half smile and a choking noise. Lucky for him, I am a great actress. I throw my head back and laugh loudly.

"What's so funny, stupid?" Terry asks.

"Oh, nothing. You wouldn't be interested."

Terry takes a step closer, followed by his gang of idiots.

"Try me."

"Well, I was just saying to Benji here that you look really good in girl's clothing."

"Huh?"

"That jacket used to be mine. But it seems to fit you really well in the shoulders."

Terry's moronic friends look at each other and snicker under their breath, too scared to laugh out loud. Terry looks from them to me and back again.

"Whatever. This isn't a girl's coat," he says, but he looks unsure.

I shrug. "Whatever you say, Terry. It really brings out the blue in your eyes."

Terry's nostrils flare like a bull's and for a second I wonder if maybe I've gone too far. But then he unzips the jacket and flings it to the ground, kicking it into a pile of slush.

"Freak," he spits, glaring at Benji. "Only someone like *you* would wear a girl's coat."

Terry walks over Benji's coat as he leaves, careful to grind it deeper into the dirty snow. One after another, Terry's friends follow behind him, adding their own muddy footprints. When they're gone, Benji fishes his jacket out of the puddle with a stick. It's too wet and too dirty to put on.

"We can wash it at my house after school," I offer.

Benji nods.

"Ahoy there, mateys!" Bundled up in a puffy jacket, Harry Potter scarf and a huge hat with ear flaps, Mr. Campbell is instantly recognizable. No other teacher has less style. "Tad cold to be out without a jacket on, Mr. Denton."

Benji shrugs, but it's hard to tell under all that shivering.

I look meaningfully at his jacket, dripping off the stick.

"It would be even colder if he put it on," I say.

"Good grief! What were you doing, ice fishing?"

This is normally the sort of lame joke that would make Benji smile, but Terry DiCarlo has a way of ruining even the lamest of jokes for him. That plus the cold have rendered him speechless, and he just stares miserably at his feet.

Loud laughter makes us all turn around. Over by the tire swing, Terry DiCarlo is doing his Benji impressions again. Benji shifts his weight from one foot to the other. He looks positively blue.

"Sir Benjamin, why don't you head on in early? If you hang your coat over the radiator it should dry out before you head home for the day. Here's the washroom pass; you can go get yourself set up for math."

Benji takes the pass from Mr. Campbell and scurries toward the portable, taking his coat on a stick with him.

"Should I go with him?" I ask.

"Mr. Denton knows his way," Mr. Campbell says. "But perhaps you could fill me in on what I missed?"

Everything, I want to say. That's the problem. Teachers miss everything. If I tell him what really happened, then Terry and company will know I ratted them out and they'll make it even worse for Benji. Where was Mr. Campbell when Benji's locker was broken into, or when his coat was being trampled? It shouldn't be my job to clue him in on what's been happening right in front of his eyes. He's the teacher, not me.

When it becomes clear that I have nothing more to say, Mr. Campbell sighs and says, "It seems you've been struck with selective amnesia. Well, if you remember something, I hope you'll come to me."

Doubtful.

Betsy Blue

After school Benji and I are walking home, trying to guess which people in our class will be invited to Min's birthday, when Benji points across the street and says, "Hey, isn't that Betsy Blue?"

Betsy Blue is the name of our car. My mother has called it by that name for as long as I can remember. Sure enough, Betsy Blue is parked under a tree across from the school and mom is sitting behind the wheel, biting her nails, even though she knows Denise will give her heck for it later.

"What's she doing here?" Benji asks. "Do you have a dentist appointment or something?"

"I don't think so," I say.

As we're crossing the street, Mom looks up and spots us. She smiles and waves us in.

"What are you doing here?" I demand, climbing into the front seat. "How come you're not at work?"

Mom starts the car and heads toward home. "I didn't have any clients this afternoon, so I thought I'd pick you up."

I frown. It's Friday afternoon; there are always clients on Friday afternoons. People like to get their hair cut so they can be fresh and cute for the weekend.

"That's weird," I say, but if she hears me, she doesn't acknowledge it.

"Benji, is it all right if I drop you off at home? Clarissa and I have some errands to do."

"Sure."

"Can't he come with us?" I ask.

"Not this time, Clarissa."

Something weird is going on. Benji is practically my brother. Sometimes I think Mom likes him more than she likes me. She's always going on about his manners and work ethic and what a sweet kid he is. He comes over practically every day, even Christmas. What kind of errands do we have to do that he can't come along for? Maybe I do have an appointment I forgot about. Now that I think about it, I can't remember the last time I saw the eye doctor, or the dentist for that matter.

Mom pulls up in front of Benji's house. "Have a nice evening, hon. Say hello to your dad for me."

Mom smiles at him in the rear-view mirror.

I watch Benji get out of the car and trudge up his front stairs. He turns around once to wave. Mom backs out of the driveway and heads downtown. The health complex is in the opposite direction.

"Where are we going?" I ask.

"I thought I'd take you for ice cream," Mom says.

"Why couldn't Benji come then?"

"Just us girls today," Mom says. "We have some things to discuss."

"Like what?"

"Let's wait till we get our ice cream. How was school today?"

But I don't want to talk about school. Why is my mother

taking me out for ice cream on a Friday afternoon when I know very well we have frozen yogurt in the freezer at home?

There aren't very many people at the Dairy Queen, which isn't all that surprising, since it's late November and it's getting much colder. Not that the temperature matters to me. Personally, I've never understood why people don't eat ice cream in the winter. Just because it's cold outside doesn't make it any less delicious.

"Order anything you like," Mom says.

"Anything?" I ask.

"Anything."

I order a banana split with the works: three scoops of ice cream, chocolate, caramel and strawberry sauce, peanuts, whip cream and sprinkles. Mom gets a baby vanilla cone. I go to sit in a booth by the window, but Mom wants to sit closer to the back.

"It's too loud up there," she says. "Too many people."

So we sit at a table in the very back, near the back door. There's a bit of a draft, so I keep my coat on. I dig into my split, trying to make sure every spoonful has a little bit of everything in each bite. It's a lot harder than you'd think. Sometimes I have to use my finger to scoop a peanut or a bit of sauce on top.

"Clarissa, I have something to tell you, and I'm just going to say it. I want you to listen and not say anything until I'm done. Then you can ask anything you want. Can you do that?"

What kind of a question is that? Apparently my own mother thinks I am an imbecile incapable of hearing some-one out.

"Can you do that?" she asks again.

I nod.

"I want to hear you say yes, I can do that."

"Yes, I can do that," I say, rolling my eyes and licking caramel sauce off my plastic spoon.

"I picked you up today on my way home from the hospital. I had a meeting with an oncologist, Dr. Fairbanks."

The hospital?

"An oncologist is a doctor who specializes in cancer. Clarissa, honey, I've been diagnosed with breast cancer."

Mom stops and watches me, letting the words sink in. I wait for the punch line. It has to be a joke. Not a very funny one, but then again most of Mom's jokes are pretty lame. The ice cream hardens in my throat. I manage to force it down, but I don't take another bite.

Mom continues, "Dr. Fairbanks says there is no reason to panic, as they caught it at an early stage. I'm going to have surgery in a few weeks, followed by chemotherapy. I've asked Denise to come stay with us for awhile, to help out while I'm recovering."

"Denise knows?"

"Clarissa, I asked you not to interrupt. Yes, Denise knows. She is my best friend. I asked her to come to the hospital with me. Sometimes you need another adult with you. I didn't want to worry you until I knew what was going on."

I want to tell her to slow down, start from the beginning. I hear all the things she's saying, but they don't make any sense. Her lips are still moving but my brain can't seem to catch up.

"I'll be working up until my surgery, and then I'll have to take some time off. The General Hospital doesn't have a cancer ward, and so I'll be staying in London while I get my chemotherapy."

Cancer? Surgery? London? Denise? Chemotherapy? There are so many things I want to shout, but I can't. I don't even know where to start. I can't believe that only ten feet away people are trying to decide whether to get a chocolate-dipped cone or a small Blizzard, completely unaware that my whole life is changing. Five minutes ago I was just like them, and now all of a sudden I'm a person whose mother has cancer.

"I know you're overwhelmed, and you must have lots of questions. But I just needed to get it all out first. Now, ask me anything you want. Anything."

Unbelievably, Mom is smiling at me. I recognize that smile, it's the one she gives to little kids who don't want to get their hair cut; the one she uses to charm them into letting her take her scissors to their head and chop away to her heart's content. Well, she's not coming anywhere near me with that smile, I know what she's up to. I will not be talked down to. She reaches for my hand, but I pull it back. I don't like being touched in public. She *knows* that.

"It's important to talk about this, honey."

I open my mouth to speak, but instead of words, ice cream comes rushing up my throat and I puke all over the table.

***

At home, Mom lays a bunch of pamphlets at the edge of my bed, Cancer in the Family, Breast Cancer FAQs, Cancer is a Word, Not a Sentence.

"I thought you might want to look at these," she explains. "In case you have any questions you're too embarrassed to ask. Next week we're going to see Dr. Fairbanks, you can ask him anything you like then."

"We?"

"He thinks it's important for you to come along."

I wait until she leaves before tossing the brochures in the garbage can.

Blocked ID

Benji calls around seven.

"Wanna come over?" he asks.

"I don't know."

"My dad's not here. He went to a hockey game."

"Maybe."

"We can watch TV."

"There's nothing good on Friday nights."

"He left money for pizza."

"Fine. But no mushrooms."

"Can't you just pick them off?"

"No, I can still taste them."

"What if I ask them just to put mushrooms on half?"

"Fine."

"Okay, see you soon?"

"I'm coming right now. I'll bring pop."

Mom is in her room on the phone, probably spreading the bad news. I wonder who she's talking to, and why they have to know our business. I put my coat on, stuff two cans of root beer into the pockets and wait till I'm practically out the door before yelling, "I'm going to Benji's!" Then I slam the door behind me and run to Benji's before she can say anything back.

Benji is waiting for me at the door. He frowns as I burst into the house, gasping for breath.

"Did you run here?" he asks.

I can't answer right away because I'm trying to catch my breath.

"What does it look like?"

"You never run."

"I do so, just not in gym class. Did you order the pizza?"

"Yup. If it's not here in thirty-five more minutes, then it's free."

"Great. Here's your root beer. Anything good on TV?"

Benji's house is set up exactly like mine. All the rooms are in the same place, except at Benji's, nothing matches. David Denton has been married twice, and neither of those women was around long enough to spiff the place up a bit. Benji's mom died in a car accident when he was only two, and his ex-stepmom Gayle wasn't really the decorating type. Or the mom type, come to think of it. She was the bingo-playing, heavy-smoking, soap opera-watching type. She's been gone for four years and their basement still smells like cigarettes. The worst thing about Gayle was that she hated dogs, and used to say terrible things under her breath whenever a dog walked by or started barking outside, almost like she was cursing them. We used to call her the Gulch, like Miss Gulch, the mean lady in *The Wizard of Oz* who wants to hurt Toto. the Gulch could be really fun, but she didn't like much of anything and spent most of her time complaining. We could talk about the Gulch right in front of her and she never got it. I guess she wasn't the smart type, either.

The only room that's really put together is Benji's room, but we never hang out in there because it's pretty small and he doesn't like things to get mussed up. We usually end up in the basement. David has a big TV with over five hundred channels, surround sound and one of those extra-long corner couches that looks expensive but is really made of fake leather. He has a real leather La-Z-Boy, but we're not allowed to sit on it. Not that I care. Who'd want to sit in an old chair when you can spread out over a whole couch? At Benji's, you can turn the TV up as loud as you want and no one tells you to turn it down. But even with all this cool stuff, Benji still would rather be at my house. He says it gets too quiet here.

"Wanna watch a movie?" he asks.

"Sure. But you figure it out. I can never get the thingy to work."

Benji picks up one of three remote controls and a menu pops up with all the different movie choices. Most of them are Oscar types. Boring.

"Can you find something funny?" I ask.

"I'll try," Benji says.

While he wades through the long list of movies, I think about Mom and whether I want to tell Benji about the C word. Mom told me that I should, but I don't know if I want to. He'll probably get upset and cry and I hate when people cry. Plus he might want to talk about it, and I don't want to talk about it. I'm not sure it's even real. How can you tell someone you have the C word and then come home like everything is normal and blab on the phone to your friends all night? Maybe it will go away on its own, like when some people get the flu they are sick for days and other people get over it in twenty-four hours. How can I tell Benji about it when we don't really know for sure, *for sure*, yet? I'd be worrying him for nothing.

The doorbell rings and I jump up.

"I'll get it, where's the money?"

"On the counter," Benji says.

Pizza makes everything better. There is nothing that a hot slice of cheesy-tomatoey goodness can't fix, especially with lots of salty pepperoni. Delicious. I scarf down three slices before Benji asks about this afternoon.

"Did you have a doctor's appointment?"

"No."

"Dentist?"

"No."

I reach for my fourth slice. I am not about to let a bunch of Nosy-Parker questions ruin a good pizza.

"Was it about your dad?"

I hadn't even thought about my dad. Talk about a perfect cover story; Benji would be too embarrassed to ask a lot of questions, and he'd never have to know about my mom. It would be a pretty big lie to tell though, and although I have nothing against lying, I've never been able to lie to Benji.

"No."

Benji puts his pizza down and looks at me very seriously. He takes a deep breath before asking, "Are you moving?"

"No. It's nothing like that," I say, but I can tell that he doesn't believe me.

"You don't want to tell me," Benji says. He looks disappointed.

"It's just not important enough. I don't want to worry you." Benji looks alarmed.

"If it's not important, why would I be worried?" he asks.

This is going all wrong.

"It's just my mom. She has to go see a doctor."

"Why?"

71

"Because she might—" but I can't bring myself to say it out loud.

"Die?" Benji whispers.

"Cripes! Don't be so dramatic! It's just, I mean she might have—" I lower my voice before finishing, "cancer."

There. I said it. Benji is staring at me like I said she had to have a face transplant or something unbelievable like that. When he speaks his voice is hushed, too.

"Cancer?"

I shrug.

"Maybe."

"What do you mean, maybe?"

"Well, this one doctor thinks so, but she's acting like it's nothing, and she doesn't seem sick, so maybe he was wrong. She's going to see another doctor next week."

"Okaaaay," Benji says, "but one doctor already said she had it?"

"Yeah, so? She needs a second opinion. People are always getting second opinions." At least on TV they are.

"What kind is it?"

A red hot flush rushes up my neck and spreads across my cheeks.

"Can we please talk about something else? You're ruining my pizza."

"Sorry, it's just, wow. Cancer. I've never known anyone with cancer before."

"*Maybe* cancer."

"Maybe cancer. I'm sorry, Clarissa."

"What are you sorry for? You didn't do anything. Besides, I said I wasn't talking about it anymore."

"Right. Sorry."

We chew in silence until I can't stand it anymore. I can

practically hear Benji feeling sorry for me. That won't do at all.

"So did you get the thingy to work?" I ask.

Benji nods. "Yup."

"So what are we watching?"

"*Miss Congeniality.*"

On a scale of one to five, I'd only give *Miss Congeniality* two stars. But Benji loves anything with a makeover in it, and I'll do anything to keep him distracted enough to forget about my mom, so *Miss Congeniality* it is.

***

A little bit later the phone rings. Benji answers. After a second he hangs up.

"Who was that?" I ask.

Benji shrugs.

"Wrong number," he says.

Ten seconds later the phone rings again. Benji looks at it but doesn't make a move to answer.

"Aren't you going to get that?" I ask.

He shrugs.

"It's probably the same people."

"What if it's for your dad?"

Benji hesitates and picks it up on the fourth ring.

"Hello?"

This time he hangs up right away.

"Same guy?"

He nods but doesn't say a word. When the phone rings for the third time he doesn't even look at it. This is starting to get annoying.

"Cripes!"

"Just leave it," he says.

"They probably wrote the number down wrong. Here, I'll get it."

Benji puts an arm out to stop me but I've always been way stronger than him. I grab the phone and check out the number, but the screen says blocked ID.

"Benji, what are you doing? Let me get the phone!"

"It's not worth it, let's just watch the movie."

"Hello?"

"Don't hang up on me, freak! What's the matter? You on a date with a boy? Are you doing each other's hair? Playing dress up?"

"Who is this?" I demand.

But no one answers. There's a click and then the drone of the dial tone buzzing in my ear. Benji turns up the TV and pretends to be totally engrossed in Sandra Bullock and her silly beauty pageant antics.

"Have you got phone calls like that before?" I ask.

Benji feigns surprise. "Like what?" he says.

"Don't be stupid, Benji. Do they call here a lot?"

"Was it a wrong number?"

"Cripes, Benji! Does your dad know?"

Benji pales, but he refuses to tear his eyes from the TV screen.

"Of course not. And don't tell him. He'd just get angry."

I grab the remote and turn off the TV.

"Why didn't you tell me about the phone calls?"

"You weren't going to tell me about your mom."

"That's different!" I explode. "That's personal! This is, this is—" but I can't think of an appropriate word.

"They're just crank calls," Benji says.

"So? I still think you should tell your dad. No one would ever call here again after the Dentonator gave them an earful."

"He'd probably think I brought it on myself."

"No he wouldn't," I protest, but part of me knows that Benji is right.

"Can we please turn the movie back on now?" he asks.

I'm far too angry to sit still and watch a movie, but Benji looks so pitiful that I can't say no. Try as I might, I can't get back into the plot. My mind feels like it's racing a hundred miles an hour. I can't get that ugly voice out of my head, and I wonder if there is anything else Benji isn't telling me.

Bombarded

"Don't forget, Clarissa, straight home after school today. We have a meeting with Dr. Fairbanks at 3:45."

I pretend to be busy looking for something in my backpack.

"Did you hear me, Clarissa?"

"*Mmm, hmm,*" I mumble.

Mom crosses her arms and leans to one side.

"Then what did I say?" she asks.

"You said be home before 3:45."

"That's not exactly what I said, but you got the gist of it."

Benji arrives and knocks politely on the screen door. I don't know why he insists on doing this, since the front door is open and he can see us standing right there. Plus, it's not like he's a total stranger or hasn't been coming to my house every day for the past five years anyway. I wonder if there's such a thing as *too* polite.

"Hi, Clarissa. Hello, Miss Delaney."

"Are you ever going to call me Annie?"

"Right. Annie. Sorry."

Benji licks his lips and shifts his weight from foot to foot.

"How are you feeling?" he asks.

My mom smiles.

"I'm feeling okay, Benji, thanks for asking. I'm glad Clarissa told you about the diagnosis and I just want you to know that things look good. Plenty of women are diagnosed with breast cancer every day and live to tell about it."

Benji blushes when she says the B word. I hadn't told him what kind of cancer it was to spare him (and me) the embarrassment. A gentle soul like Benji embarrasses easily, but Mom doesn't seem to notice. She keeps barrelling on with more and more embarrassing statistics.

"The important thing is we caught it early and we're going to do everything we can to beat it. The doctor told me that one in nine women will develop breast cancer in her lifetime. It's the most common cancer among women. Even men can get breast cancer. Can you imagine—"

"We're going to be late," I say. "Benji, let's go."

"Bye Miss — Annie."

"Bye, Benji. Clarissa, I'll see you no later than 3:30."

I stomp out the door, slamming it behind me. Benji struggles to catch up.

He looks a little shaken.

"Sorry," I say. "It's all she can talk about these days."

"It's okay."

"No, it's not okay! She's embarrassing me! She's embarrassing my friends."

"I don't mind, really."

"Well, I do."

"Wouldn't you rather know what's going on?"

"No, I wouldn't. I don't want to go see the stupid doctor."

"I would."

"Well it's not your mother, is it?"

As soon as it's out of my mouth, I regret it. Mother comments are below the belt where Benji is concerned.

"Sorry," I grumble. "It just makes me so mad."

A terrible thought comes over me, a thought that makes my skin go cold and clammy, like I'm going to be sick. I stop dead in my tracks and turn to Benji.

"You're not going to tell anyone, are you?" I ask.

Benji looks truly shocked.

"Of course not!"

"Good. Because if you did—"

But I don't need to finish that sentence. We both know I could cream him if I really wanted to.

***

I arrive home promptly at 3:30 to find Mom and Denise waiting for me in the car.

"What is *she* doing here?"

"It's nice to see you, too, kiddo."

"*Denise* is here because I want her to be involved. She is like family to me, so you can check that attitude at the door."

I climb into the car — the back seat, since Denise's horse legs are so long she has to sit in the front — slip on my sunglasses and slink as far down in my seat as possible. I don't want anyone to see me arriving at the hospital and spread rumours.

Dr. Fairbanks' office is inside the hospital, which I have only been in once, not counting when I was born there, because who remembers their own birth? Two years ago I fell off the monkey bars and broke my wrist. Ever since then I have turned my back on a career as an acrobat in Cirque du Soleil and sworn off monkey bars and hospitals in general.

I hate going to the hospital. The nurses and doctors talk in hushed voices and then take you behind green curtains to whisper about more bad news. It's too quiet. It feels like the whole building is holding its breath, and any minute the doors will burst open and all these stretchers will roll in carrying people screaming in pain and bleeding all over the place. I tell my mom this, but she says I've seen too many TV hospital dramas and that a disaster of that scale is highly unlikely.

"But it could happen," I protest.

"Yes, Clarissa, it *could* happen, but it's highly unlikely."

"But it *could*."

"Yes, it could. But if it did, I doubt they would bring them up to the cancer clinic."

"I wouldn't mind being tended to by George Clooney or Patrick Dempsey," Denise says.

"In my experience, real doctors never have such great hair," Mom sighs. "They're usually balding."

Denise laughs, maybe a little too loudly, because the receptionist frowns at us over the edge of her glasses and the woman across from us looks up from her magazine as if we were swearing at each other at the top of our lungs.

"*Shhh*," Mom whispers. "No laughing in the hospital," which of course makes them laugh harder.

If you ask me, the hospital could use a lot more laughing.

***

"Dr. Fairbanks will see you now, Annie."

Even though the receptionist isn't speaking directly to me, my heart starts leaping around in my chest.

"That's us, girls."

Mom stands up, gathers her coat, purse and nail file and heads down the hall into Dr. Fairbank's office like she's headed for just a regular checkup at your run of the mill doctor's office. She looks impossibly beautiful. How can she be sick? Denise and I follow behind her. I think Denise might be even more nervous than I am, since she just popped her fourth piece of gum in less than half an hour. The sound of her jaw popping as she chomps away is driving me crazy. I will have to make sure that Mom sits in the middle in Dr. Fairbank's office.

"Ah. Welcome. Annie, Denise good to see you again, and you must be Clarissa."

Well, Mom was right about the bald doctor thing. Dr. Fairbanks has a perfectly round bald patch on the top of his head, surrounded by a thinning ring of brown hair. He's short, chubby round the middle and his cheeks are pink, even though it's not cold enough for them to look so rosy. His hand, when I shake it, is warm and dry, with a wedding ring wedged onto his fourth finger. Too bad, Denise.

"Today we are here to talk about Annie's treatment schedule, but do you have any questions first?"

We all shake our heads.

He takes a pair of glasses out of the chest pocket of his lab coat and rests them on the edge of his nose.

"We're going to start by removing the lump and some of the surrounding cells, followed by chemotherapy and eventually radiation therapy, which will zap any of the remaining cancerous cells in the area."

I try to imagine what that might look like, and I picture one of those arcade games with the guns that you point at the screen to shoot blinking lights. Now all I can think about is Dr. Fairbanks and a team of nurses wearing goggles and masks and pointing laser guns at my mother's chest.

"The actual treatment won't hurt at all, but it can cause redness and tenderness of the breast."

"So can breastfeeding," Mom says.

Oh god. I feel my cheeks flushing and I sink lower into my chair as Denise and Dr. Fairbanks laugh. I don't see what's so funny.

"A sense of humour is so important," Dr. Fairbanks says. "I can see you've got that in spades."

"Now, you'll be seeing a radiologist in a few weeks to determine the length of your treatment, but as we discussed, we don't have the facilities here at the General Hospital. The closest centre is London. Have you considered your options?"

"I have, but we still need to iron out a few things," Mom says.

Options? What options?

"Do you have any questions, Clarissa?"

I shrug and avoid making eye contact. The sooner I get out of here the better.

Dr. Fairbanks continues, "A lot of kids want to know if cancer is contagious, like a cold. The answer to that is no, you can't catch cancer from another person. Another common question is whether or not someone will die. It's true that many people die from cancer, but not everyone. We're going to do everything we can to help your mother and I think she has a good chance of a complete and total recovery."

Everyone keeps telling me that they're going to do everything they can, and that they caught it early, like that makes everything better, but the fact is nothing is one-hundred percent for sure. Lots of things could still go wrong. I hate that no one seems to be taking this as seriously as I am. I want to know what happens if the cancer doesn't go away. What do we do then? Those are the questions I really want to ask, but somehow I don't think

...anks is prepared to give me.

..., and if I don't get out of here as

...ble I'll be blubbering.

"May I be excused?" I ask.

Dr. Fairbanks blinks. "Excused?" he repeats.

"To go to the bathroom," I add.

His face relaxes into a smile.

"Of course. I have a few more things to discuss with you mother, though. Would you like us to wait—"

"Oh, no," I interrupt. "Don't wait; you can continue. I'll just wait outside."

"Just ask Judy at reception to point you in the right direction," Dr. Fairbanks says. I nod but don't look back. I can feel my mother's eyes boring into me. She knows I'm lying about the bathroom but I don't care. If I stay here one more second I'll scream.

***

I wish I could say that the rest of the visit was a breeze, but it wasn't. While I was waiting, minding my own business, the woman next to me started telling me about her husband John and his colon. I wasn't exactly sure what a colon was but I had a fuzzy idea that it was something disgusting, maybe even more embarrassing than the B word, which is a word I hope I never have to say out loud. It is definitely not something you would talk to perfect strangers about, but try telling that to Susan. She had no problem telling me all about her husband's colon and how he was a stage one, "Thank the Lord," and how they were about to begin treatments.

I nodded politely without ever looking up from *National Geographic*. I don't even like science magazines but anything was better than talking about colons with Susan. Besides, they had an article about blue whales that was almost interesting.

After she ran out of colon-related things to tell me, Susan asked why a young girl like me was sitting in a hospital on such a nice day. I find it very annoying that adults are always telling you to be polite and not ask nosy questions but this rule doesn't seem to apply to them. I wish I could fake deafness, or at least a fainting spell, but when the moment strikes I always seem to lose my nerve.

"I'm waiting for my mom."

Susan's eyes went all big behind her glasses, and for a minute I was seriously worried that she was about to pull me into a hug. I scooched over in my seat and coughed into my hand. With any luck she would think I had some sort of contagious bug. She looked like the type to carry Purell in her bag and wipe off doorknobs with Wet-Naps. She was wearing pink granny pants with a matching blouse and had a no-nonsense frosty gray bob with poufy bangs, the kind of hair my mom called safety-helmet head. Helmet because of its shape, and safe because there was nothing stylish or controversial about it.

"You poor child. What kind of cancer does she have?"

If only I could cry on cue. Then Susan would feel so bad about hounding me about my mother's cancer, she would let it go. But the thought of saying the B word aloud still couldn't bring tears to my eyes. This was one of the only times I wish I could trade places with Mattie Cohen. Crying is one of her better talents.

I became aware of Susan staring at me. She leaned in and patted my knee, murmuring things like, "there, there" and "poor child." We were dangerously close to hugging territory.

Susan was so close I could smell her perfume. Definitely Wild n' Freesia. It smelled thick and sweet and made my nose hairs tingle, like cheap hairspray. I could either spit the word out or suffocate in her old lady perfume.

My cheeks were so hot I thought for a moment that maybe I really was getting sick. Susan didn't seem to notice how uncomfortable I was. Or maybe she thought I was upset. She was cooing and shaking her head.

"It must be hard for you to talk about. You brave, brave girl. You'll be in my prayers. You and your mother."

And then she grabbed my hand and gave it a squeeze. I managed to mumble a thank you and tried to pull my hand away, but Susan continued to hold it until her husband returned from the examining room. He seemed like a nice man. He had a bit of a stoop and a nice smile, the shy kind. He reminded me a little of Benji. When he came in, Susan jumped up and got his coat for him. I flexed my hand, which was numb from being squeezed so tightly, and resumed flipping through my *National Geographic*. While Susan had held my hand captive, I had been stuck on the same page for ten minutes.

I wondered if maybe I should say something to John, but I didn't know what to say. Good luck with your colon sounded like a joke, even though I really meant it. Instead I kept my head down and pretended to be fascinated by pygmy nuthatches. When I looked up, Susan and her husband were gone.

Breast

Of all the cancers in the world, my mother had to get breast cancer. I don't even like to think about the B word, let alone say it. Just the thought of saying it out loud makes my voice box shrivel up like a raisin and my cheeks burn. As if the B word itself wasn't bad enough, now every time I hear it I will immediately think "cancer," like in that game where someone says a word and you blurt out the first thing that comes to mind. For example, if you say "full," Benji will shout "house" out so fast, it's almost like he knew what you were going to say before you said it. He loves that dumb show that much.

Today alone I had to say the B word four times. That is more than I have said it aloud in my entire life.

The first three times I was in the guidance counsellor's office, sitting across from Mrs. Stremecki who thought it would be a good idea to talk about my mother's illness. I don't know how schools find out all these private things about you. In this case I imagine my mother made a phone call, requesting someone deal with her difficult daughter. Unfortunately Mrs. Stremecki is one of those people who thinks that in order to overcome something you have to confront it by verbalizing it. She seems to think that the

VIKKI VanSICKLe

more I am able to say the words "breast cancer," the more equipped I will be for dealing with it, like if I can say the words aloud, I won't be afraid of what they mean. I swear, she tried to squeeze the B word in as many times as possible.

"Tell me how you feel about your mother's breast cancer."

"Do you have any questions about breast cancer?"

"Are you worried you might lose your mother to breast cancer?"

I crossed my arms tight across my body and answered in as few words as possible. Mom calls this my Sullen Sally act but Mrs. Stremecki didn't seem to find it as exasperating as she does. Obviously she thought it was due to my mother's cancer, and because she is a guidance counsellor, it is probably written right into her contract that she has to be more sensitive than most parents.

"We can talk about this later, Clarissa, but I want you to know that my door is always open if you need me."

I nodded and thanked her, but before she let me go, I had to say the words "breast cancer" three times. When I was done she gave my shoulder a squeeze and sent me back to geography with a sucker, which did not make up for the fact that I had to say the B word out loud three times, even if it was grape.

The fourth and absolute worst time was in language arts. Mrs. Stremecki had kept me longer than I had thought, and so when I returned to Mr. Campbell's class, they were finished with geography and had moved on to reading circles. I handed my slip to Mr. Campbell without looking at him and slid into my seat. I knew that if I looked at him he would be able to tell that I had spent thirty minutes in the guidance office talking about, well, you know. I squeaked past teacher-interrogation, but I wasn't so lucky when it came to my group members.

"Where were you?" Rocco demanded.

I ignored him, as I always ignore anything Rocco Martinez says. He always has a runny nose and runs around burping in people's faces. Normally everyone else ignores Rocco, too, except this time my group seemed to be looking at me, waiting for an answer.

"Yeah, where were you?" Kevin repeated.

"It's none of your business—"

"She was in guidance. I saw her."

I swear if I could have any super power it would be laser eyes so I could have killed Amanda Krespi with one look. Rocco got all excited. Probably because he is usually the one spending time with Mrs. Stremecki.

"Guidance? Really? Are you failing?"

"No, I am *not* failing."

Rocco looked confused. "Are your parents getting divorced or something?"

Amanda frowned and elbowed him sharply in the side. "No, stupid, Clarissa doesn't have a dad."

"I do so have a dad, Amanda."

"Well you don't *live* with him or anything."

"Excuse me, but if you *don't mind*, I'd like to work on the book—"

"Come on, you can tell us!" Kevin begged.

I shrugged, like it was no big deal, and opened my book to chapter three, but I felt them all staring at me and I knew there was no way to get out of it. I considered raising my hand and asking for the sick pass, but then my whole group would have talked about me while I was gone, Amanda and Mattie would have gone on about it more at lunch and pretty soon the whole class would be whispering about my big secret.

"Guys, leave her alone. I'm sure she doesn't want to talk about it." Mattie smiled at me across the table. I smiled back and thought, she isn't always so bad.

"Besides, you wouldn't want people bothering you if your mother had cancer."

I was not smiling anymore. Neither was anyone else. Rocco actually dropped his pencil and Kevin suddenly, for the first time ever, became interested in his workbook. Amanda's mouth fell open and she looked from me to Mattie and back to me again.

"Does she really, Clarissa?"

Mattie tossed her stupid perfect hair, annoyed that anyone would dare to second guess her. "Of course she does. My mom's a nurse and she talked to her at the hospital last week." Then she looked at me all concerned and said, "I'm very sorry, Clarissa."

"Is it bad? Like, is she going to die?" Rocco asked.

"Rocco!" Mattie pretended to be shocked but I don't know why she'd be surprised. She's the one who'd brought it up.

"What kind of cancer is it?" Amanda asked. "My grandpa died of lung cancer."

"It's none of your business." I snapped.

"Skin cancer?"

"No."

"Brain cancer?"

"No."

"Arm cancer?"

Mattie rolled her eyes and made a disgusted noise. "There's no such thing as arm cancer, Rocco. How stupid can you be?"

"I'm NOT stupid, idiot!"

"If we guess it, will you say it?" Kevin asked.

"No, no, no!"

I searched wildly for Mr. Campbell, but he was on the other side of the room with Benji's group, laughing at something, totally unaware that one of his students was being tortured only a few metres away.

"It's a lady cancer," Mattie whispered.

I imagined my laser eyes cutting her into a thousand little pieces, which I would then put in an envelope and mail to her mother with a note saying, *Dear Mrs. Cohen, This is what happens to people who can't keep their big mouths shut. You're next.*

"You mean—" Rocco cupped his hands over his chest and batted his eyelashes.

Kevin snickered and made kissy faces.

Mattie gasped. "That is rude and inappropriate!"

Amanda's hand shot into the air. "I'm telling!"

"Is everything okay, group four?"

Mr. Campbell looked over, finally — along with the rest of the class.

"*Shhh!*" I hissed.

"Amanda?"

Amanda took her hair out of her mouth long enough to whine, "Mr. Campbell, Rocco is being rude and sexist."

"Is that so, Rocco?"

Rocco dropped his hands and shook his head. "No."

"Will someone tell me what he was doing? Clarissa?"

I shook my head and stared down at my notebook.

"Does that mean you don't know, or you won't tell?"

I shrugged.

"Use your words, please, Clarissa. Expression is a wonderful thing."

At this point, I'm not sure who I hate more. Mattie Cohen or Mr. Campbell.

Somehow I managed to unstick my throat and say, "He was doing something rude with his hands."

"What was he doing?" Mr. Campbell pressed.

"He was making — I mean he pretended his hands were—" I looked desperately at Amanda and Mattie for help. Amanda looked down at her book and chewed her hair and Mattie had worked herself up to a state of tears. So much for sisterhood.

"Yes, Clarissa?"

"He was pretending his hands were — you know." I shrugged and looked down at my own chest, my cheeks flaming. If it were possible to die of embarrassment, I'd be dead right now.

Mr. Campbell smiled his big toothy smile and shrugged. "I'm afraid I don't. He was pretending his hands were . . ."

"Breasts."

I said it as quiet as humanly possible but it wasn't quiet enough. Giggles popped up around the room like mushrooms after a rainstorm. Mr. Campbell cleared his throat and tried to gain control over the situation but the damage had been done. The entire seventh-grade class had heard me say the B word. There was a buzzing in my ears that I'm sure is some sort of primitive defence mechanism that helps people survive complete and utter mortification. It must have worked, because here I am.

***

"We have to do something about Mr. Campbell, Benji."

"Why?"

"Because I hate him! He thinks he's so smart and so

funny, but I can't spend a whole year listening to Tony the Tiger! We were supposed to have Miss Ross! It's not fair!"

"What should we do?"

"Well, no one will listen to us; we're just two lowly students. And my mom won't get involved, she's always going on about how life is unfair and you need to learn how to deal with it. Denise is obviously out of the question, but what about your dad? Everyone knows the Dentonator."

"I don't know. He doesn't really get involved with school much."

"Benji, think!"

He looks offended.

"I am thinking," he says.

"Well, think harder. We have to come up with something quick. I don't think I can stand it much longer. This is our number one concern right now."

Benji gives me a funny look.

"What about your mom?" he asks.

I glare at him, daring him to say anything more.

"What about her? I already said she won't be any help," I say firmly.

Benji squirms.

"Okay. I'll think about it."

Blame

The answer to our problem walks into the Hair Emporium a week later.

Benji and I are crouched behind the Japanese screen playing one of my favourite games, Whose Shoes. We created it one day when we discovered you could still see people's feet coming down the stairs to the salon through the gap at the bottom of the screens. The point of the game was to guess who the client was by her shoes. At first we almost never got anybody right, so instead we decided to make up characters to fit the shoes. Like the purple cowboy boots with the ratty looking fringe, maybe they belonged to a country singer who was in town hiding from her crazy husband with a bad temper. How disappointing it was to find out that they really belonged to Mrs. Gregorio, the drama teacher at the high school. So now whenever I meet someone I make sure to check out their shoes, kind of like research.

For example, Denise only wears high heels, at least two inches, usually with pointy toes. She says that as a sales woman, her appearance is part of the package, "and I make a much better package in heels." But then she complains about how sore her feet are at the end of the day. She is forever rubbing them and moaning about her corns and bunions and calluses. I try very hard not to look at her feet when she says these things. I have never seen a corn or a bunion and I hope to keep it that way. She says it's because she spends all day on her feet, but I think it's because she spends all day in high heels. My mother spends all day on her feet and you don't hear her complaining. Of course, she gets those white running shoes that nurses wear. That is because my mother is sensible and Denise is not.

Today we're waiting for the next customer when the door opens and an unfamiliar pair of expensive but practical-looking boots (brown leather, with a medium heel and salt stains on the toe) comes walking down the stairs.

"She is an Alaskan movie star who just got back from a shoot in the Arctic," Benji whispers.

"No, no. She's a descendent of Viking hunters who made their fortune hunting and selling polar bear hides, and she's just come back from a hunting trip."

The Alaskan movie star/bear hunter spoils our fun by peering around the Japanese screen. She's younger and far more glamorous than most of the clients at the Hair Emporium, with her long woollen coat, leather gloves and some kind of designer bag tucked under her arm.

"Hi, I'm Marion McKinnon. I have a hair appointment at four," she says.

"You're not really supposed to be back here," I tell her, sitting back on my heels. "The waiting area is right there, on the other side of the screen."

Marion smiles at me.

"Who are you, security?" she asks.

"My name is Clarissa Delaney. My mom is the owner and sole stylist of the Hair Emporium. And this is Benji."

"I live next door," Benji offers.

"Nice to meet you Clarissa, Benji." Marion nods at each of us in turn. "So what are you doing down there on the floor?"

The nerve of some people! Before I get a chance to tell her that is, in fact, none of her business what I choose to do in my own house, Benji blurts out, "We like your boots."

Marion positively beams. People love it when you compliment their shoes. Not even Alaskan movie stars/bear hunters are immune.

"Thanks, they were in great shape until this weekend. I went up to Ottawa and they have snow already. I haven't got around to wiping off the salt stains yet."

"What's in Ottawa?" I ask.

"Besides snow?" Marion says. "There was a rally."

"Like a pep rally?" Benji asks.

Marion smiles. "More like a political rally."

Before we can find out what someone with such fancy boots was doing at a rally, my mother and Dolores Pincott appear at the salon door. Dolores is almost eighty years old and comes every Monday to get her white-almost-blue hair set in round curls all over her head. Every week she gives Benji and me a white and red striped candy from her purse. They taste like they've been there for thirty years but we don't want to hurt her feelings.

"You have a good week, Dolly, and be careful of that hip!" Mom says. She has pet names for everyone. It's one of the reasons her clients are so loyal. When you give someone a nickname, they feel special. It's like they're visiting with an old friend who just happens to be a hair stylist. She was the one who came up with Benji. He used to go by Ben, but it didn't really suit him. "Doesn't capture any of his sweetness," Mom said. Now even our teachers call him Benji. As far as I know, the only one who still calls him Ben is his father. But then again, the Dentonator doesn't go in for anything that's even a little bit sweet.

Mom helps Dolores/Dolly with her coat and then walks her up the stairs, but not before smiling over at Marion and saying, "You must be Marion. I'm Annie. I'll be with you in just a minute. Clarissa will show you in."

Benji and I spring to action, taking Marion's coat and asking if she would like a glass of water or a cup of tea.

"Tea, please," she says, sinking into one of the red chairs. I sit in the one next to her while Benji runs to get her tea.

"What were you rallying about?" I ask casually, twirling around on the chair.

"I'm part of a group that is lobbying the government for electoral reform."

"Hmm," I say, nodding to appear interested. The words lobbying, government and electoral make me think of social studies class. Who knew someone who looks so glamorous could be so boring?

"We just ended a pretty successful letter-writing campaign," she adds.

"What does that mean?" I ask, imagining a room full of people writing letters and licking stamp after stamp. Not very rally-like if you ask me.

"It means we had people write letters to the government expressing their concern about the current electoral system, and we finally sent enough letters to get their attention. Now we have an audience with the minister and have a real opportunity to effect change. Are you interested in politics, Clarissa?"

I don't really care all that much about the government part, but what really interests me is the bit about the letters. I need more information.

"So you sent in tons of letters and now you get to meet with someone?"

"Basically," Marion says. "And if we're successful, maybe we can change the way things are done in this country."

Before she can say anything more, Mom breezes in and puts her hand on my shoulder, which is her signal for "I can take it from here now."

"Marion, so nice to meet you. I trust my daughter has kept you entertained."

"We've just been talking about politics," Marion says. "It's so nice to meet a kid who's interested in government."

Mom's eyebrows rise, but only for a second.

"Yes, well, Clarissa is full of opinions," she says.

"Here's your tea, Miss McKinnon," Benji says, passing her a cup and saucer.

"Thanks, Benji. I don't know what I'd do without my hired muscle," Mom jokes.

Marion laughs and Benji blushes, looking equal parts pleased and embarrassed.

"Now, if you're going to be a big-time activist like Marion here, you'd better get to your homework," Mom says, giving me a look.

Marion shakes our hands and says, "Nice meeting you, Clarissa, Benji."

We say our goodbyes and then leave the salon as Mom asks Marion, "Now were you looking for a trim or shall we try something new?"

In the den I turn the TV up as loud as I can without Mom hollering at us to turn it down.

"I know how we're going to get rid of Mr. Campbell," I whisper.

Benji looks worried. "Get rid of him?"

"Yes. We're going to start a letter campaign."

***

"There, finished."

I sit back in the chair and marvel at my first letter staring back at me from the computer screen. It looks so professional, double-spaced and everything. Benji scoots his chair closer and peers over my shoulder.

"Let me read it. I'll check it for typos."

I give him a shove.

"Get out of here! I spell-checked it already!"

"You know, if we want to make it really professional we should use a letterhead," Benji suggests.

I frown.

"Where are we going to get one of those?"

"We could make one," Benji says. "Maybe there's a template we can use."

I'm not much of a computer genius so I let Benji search for the template while I get us a snack. Ugh. I was hoping for Oreos or maybe Ritz, but ever since the diagnosis Mom has been filling the house with healthy snacks, like raisins and carrot sticks. I'd rather starve than eat that rabbit food for snack.

"Sorry, Benji, nothing to eat. Wanna go to the 7-Eleven and get sour balls?"

"Sure," Benji says.

"How much money do you have?" I ask.

Benji shrugs. "Maybe a dollar."

"Well, I have a toonie. That'll have to do. Come on, print the letter and we can drop it off in the mailbox on the way."

"Where are we going to get a stamp?" Benji asks.

"Don't worry, I got it covered. Follow me."

I lead Benji up the stairs and into Mom's room.

"Are you sure we should be in here?" Benji whispers.

"The door was open," I explain. "If she didn't want people

to wander into her room she should have locked the door. Or at least shut it."

Mom keeps all her outgoing mail, bills and such, in a box on her desk marked *To Mail*. Right next to it is a roll of stamps. It looks like there are at least fifty on the roll, surely she won't miss one tiny little stamp. I slip the letter into an envelope, run my tongue over the edge to seal it and then press the stamp in the corner.

"Now, you find the school's address," I instruct Benji. "There should be a letter from the school around here somewhere."

"I think it's illegal to open someone's mail," Benji says.

"But we're not opening it," I reason with him. "We're not even really reading it. We're just looking at the outside. If that were illegal then every single mail carrier would be in jail right now."

This seems to calm him down.

"Here it is," Benji says.

"Do you think I should address it to Principal Donner or Mrs. Donner?" I ask.

"Maybe Mrs. Donner, then comma, then Principal," Benji suggests.

"Perfect."

I copy the address in my neatest handwriting and slip the letter carefully into the back pocket of my jeans.

"Come on, let's go."

***

I practically skip all the way to the 7-Eleven and back. It feels good to be doing something about Mr. Campbell.

"I think we should take turns writing the letters," I say, popping a yellow sour ball into my mouth.

"Why?" Benji asks.

"Because that way they'll sound different. It's more authentic."

Benji looks uncomfortable. "I don't know if I want to write any of them," he admits.

"Benji, do you want to effect change or not?"

A wrinkle appears above his nose as he frowns.

"What do you mean, effect change?"

I sigh.

"It's a political thing. You wouldn't understand. Do you want Miss Ross back or not?"

"Do you really think the letters will help?" Benji asks.

"Better than nothing. How's your sour key?"

Benji rips a big piece with his teeth and grimaces.

"A little stale," he admits. "How's your sour ball?"

I open the mail box and drop in the letter, closing and reopening the chute twice to make sure it goes all the way in.

"Never been sweeter."

***

Every time Mr. Campbell says something stupid or irritates me, I make a note in my workbook so I can refer to it later when I'm writing my latest letter. I'm getting really good at writing letters. I was reading them aloud to Benji, but he's gotten cold feet about the whole letter campaign, so lately I've been writing them after he goes home and mailing them myself. He probably thinks I've stopped.

It's good practise for when I'm an actress. Each time I pretend I'm someone else, a stay-at-home mom, a nurse, a lawyer, a real estate agent — I even pretended to be Denise once, but I never signed her name. I used lots of exclamation marks and phrases like "well I never," and "believe you me." I never sign any names, not even fake ones. Names can be looked up and checked against school records. Instead I use "anonymous" or "a concerned parent." If the school found out the names were fake, they wouldn't take the letters seriously. I use the thesaurus on the computer to find new words and make each letter sound slightly different. It makes me feel better to know that I am doing something about the problem instead of just sitting back and letting things happen like everyone else in the world.

***

"Have you chosen your modern day hero?" Benji asks.

"Not yet. You?"

Benji scratches his nose and passes his paper to me without a word, a sure sign that something is up. Across the top he has written the title *Annette Delaney: Local Wonder Woman*, with the words "wonder woman" done up in fancy lettering, just like on the comic books. Benji is a great artist, but if you tell him that he'll just shrug and tell you he's a great copier. Never one for compliments, which is good, because I sure wasn't about to give him one for this paper.

"What is this?" I demand.

Benji looks at me like I'm dumb or crazy or maybe both. "It's my essay."

"I know it's your essay, stupid. I mean, what are you doing writing about my mom?"

Benji shrugs again and clams up like he does when he's nervous, but I am not about to let him get away with that. When you have known someone almost your whole life, you don't suddenly get nervous around them unless you know you have done something wrong and are trying to get out of it.

"Well?"

"Well, first of all, she's an entrepreneur."

"So?"

"So that means she started her own business."

"I know what entrepreneur means, Benji. So what? Lots of people have their own businesses."

"And she's a single mom."

"Oh, I get it. And I'm such a difficult child, right? So it was ten times harder for her than for all the other single moms."

Benji looks a little sheepish but he doesn't exactly jump to say otherwise.

"And she's battling—"

"Don't say it!"

"—breast cancer."

"You *know* I hate that word."

"Sorry. Why are you so mad?"

"I am not mad!" I protest, but even as I say the words, I know they aren't true. I am mad, but I'm not sure why. So what if Benji chose my mom? The things he said are true. By Mr. Campbell's standards, she is a regular modern day hero. And yet all I want to do is grab Benji's essay and rip it to shreds.

"If you don't want me to hand it in, I don't have to," Benji says, but I know that's not what he wants. That is just the kind of best friend he is. I'm sorry to say that I actually consider taking him up on his offer, but only for a second. I may be a bad daughter but I am not a bad friend.

"I could do someone else," Benji continues. "Like Oprah."

"Don't be stupid, you're already done."

"I don't want you to be mad."

"I already told you, I'm not mad!" I snap. "I'm just — surprised."

That isn't exactly true: I am both mad and surprised. Or maybe I'm mad because I'm surprised. It never occurred to me to use my own business-owning, cancer-battling single mother as my modern day hero. She's just Mom. Someone who is always getting on my nerves and who knows just what to do to make me so angry I could scream. But Benji thought she was a hero. I went from mad to surprised to ashamed. If anyone should be writing about my mother the hero, it should be me.

"Are you going to show it to her?" I ask, hoping the answer is no. It's one thing to write about her, but to write about her AND show it to her would be too much. I would never live it down. I would forever be compared to sweet, perfect, considerate Benji.

But I shouldn't have worried. Benji pales and shakes his head. "I could never," he says, and I know it's true. He still calls her Miss Annie, for crying out loud. He'd probably faint dead away if she knew he had dedicated a whole social studies paper to her.

"Well, I won't tell," I promise, which if you think about it, is a very nice thing for me to do. Benji has so many embarrassing things to live with already; I wouldn't want to add fainting in front of his own personal hero to that list. So you see, sometimes I am not only a good friend, I am a great friend.

Bedside

On the day of Mom's surgery, Denise picks me up from school so she can drive straight to the hospital. I wish Benji could come with us but he isn't allowed to go places without the Dentonator's permission, which he probably wouldn't have given anyway. He would never let Benji get into a car with Denise. She tends to take corners a little faster than most people and has more than a few dents in her front fender to prove it.

"Call me the second you get back," he makes me promise.

"I will."

In the car, Denise is rattling off information about the surgery and how fast it is these days — how amazing medical science is. I don't say anything. If medical science is so amazing, why haven't they found a cure for cancer?

We stop in the gift shop but nothing there reminds me of Mom. In my backpack is a get-well card that Benji made this morning during health class. It's just like Benji to make something himself. I know he doesn't mean to, but he makes me look bad. I could never make a card like that. For a moment I think about not giving it to her. It's not my fault that I'm not any good at art. I browse through the cards lining the wall of the gift shop, but none of them are as good as

Benji's. Instead, I buy a bunch of magazines, add my name to the bottom of his card and vow that when I'm famous I will buy him a house with an art studio.

***

"You can see her now."

Denise gives me a push toward the nurse. She looks nice enough, a little bit like a kindergarten teacher, with a big smile — the kind that's meant to keep little kids from crying. Her dark hair is pulled back in a thick and lustrous ponytail, with zero frizz and no wisps. All-American hair, my mother would say. She's wearing pink scrubs and her running shoes are immaculately white, almost too white to be real. It makes me suspicious. I wonder if nurses have to bleach their shoes after every shift. Maybe those shoes just look white but at one time they were splattered in blood.

"You must be Clarissa," says the kindergarten nurse. "I'm Cheryl Cohen, Mattie's mom."

Dilemma. Because of Cheryl Cohen and her big mouth, my entire class knows about my mother's cancer. I have half a mind to tell her exactly what I think of big-mouthed, Nosy-Parker goody two-shoes. But now Cheryl is my mother's nurse. I can't very well be rude to her while she's looking after my mom.

"Oh," I say. "Hello." I clench my teeth to keep all the things I would like to say to her from flying out of my mouth.

Cheryl gives my shoulder a squeeze. "You're a brave girl," she says. "Mattie tells me all about you. Now come say hi to your mother. I know she wants to see you."

Inside, the room is divided into two sections by what looks like a huge green shower curtain. There's a woman sleeping in the first section, but on the other side of the curtain my mom is propped up in bed, with a tube sticking out of her arm and a glass of water resting on a food tray across her lap. She smiles when she sees me and holds out her hand. Her lips are chapped and her face is chalky white. The Annie Delaney I know would never be caught dead in public looking like that.

"Clarissa," she drawls. "Come here, baby."

Her words are slurred and she has a dopey smile on her face. I go to her and she fumbles for my hand, grabs it and pulls me to her. I'm careful not to brush against her chest in case she's still sore. I don't even want to think about what it looks like under the paper thin hospital nightie. She leans in and kisses the top of my head. She smells like the hospital, strange and antiseptic, not a trace of her coconut shampoo or perfume.

"Let me look at you." She lays a hand on each cheek and scans my face. I can't very well look away, so I study her face. She looks tired. Her skin is so pale I can see the freckles on her nose and the bags under her eyes. She keeps blinking slowly, like she's having trouble keeping her eyes open.

"Does it hurt?" I ask.

"No," she says. "I feel sort of numb."

"That's the anaesthetic," Cheryl says. "It takes awhile to get out of your system."

Mom falls back against the pillows with a sigh, still smiling that strange, loopy smile. I can't stop staring at her hands, which have fallen still on the blanket. The Annie Delaney I know is always doing something with her hands: filing her nails, twirling her hair or, most annoying of all, drumming her fingertips on the table. But these hands just lay there like something dead.

It's hot in here. I rummage around for the card, thrust it at her and mutter, "Here, we made this for you." Mom smiles and keeps blinking and for a horrible second I think she's going to cry. If she cries, I will cry, and I will not cry within ten feet of Mattie Cohen's shiny-haired mother. I can just imagine the Cohens sitting around the dinner table, clucking their tongues and shaking their heads over that poor Clarissa Delaney. There is no way I will give Mattie that satisfaction.

"I'll go get Denise," I offer, and I'm out of there lickety-split. As I leave, Cheryl Cohen squeezes my shoulder and tries to ruffle my hair, but I'm too fast for her. I glide out of there like an eagle on the wind and I don't, not even once, look back.

***

Mom was right. It doesn't take her long to get back to her bossy self. She's up and at 'em over Christmas like the surgery never happened. That day in the hospital seems so long ago, sometimes I think I must have dreamt it up, or at least exaggerated it a little. But Christmas turns into New Year's and now she's packing and getting ready for her stay at Hopestead in London, where she is scheduled to start treatment in a few days.

We have a low-key New Year's Eve party, just me, Mom, Benji and Denise, of course. It isn't much different than any other night except we wear paper crowns from leftover Christmas crackers and at midnight Mom puts a splash of champagne in our orange juice.

"My New Year's resolution is to kick cancer's ass," she says.

"I'll drink to that," Denise adds.

Beef Bourguignon

Mom is leaving today for Hopestead. She slips a key off her key chain and hands it to me, like a peace offering. "I'm giving you the key to the Hair Emporium," she says. "I want you to look after her for me. Keep her clean, air her out once in awhile. Go on, take it."

I hesitate. If I take the key, it means I accept that she is leaving me here with Denise. Still. She's not giving it to Denise, who I know would love to snoop around in there and get her big man-hands on all of the product. I take the key.

"All right," I say.

"Good girl." Mom kisses my cheek and smoothes my hair before shouldering her bag. "Denise is waiting and you need to get to school. I'll be back before you know it. You'll have so much fun you won't even miss me."

Doubtful.

"I love you."

I try to say it back to her, I *want* to say it back to her, but the words get stuck in my throat. I nod and back away into the house, throat burning. Mom catches me in a firm grip and pulls me to her anyway. She crushes me against her chest and whispers in my ear, "It's okay. You don't have to say it. I know you love me, too."

When she turns to go I rub my eyes with my sleeve, sopping up the hot tears before they make it down my cheeks.

***

No matter how hard I try, I can't concentrate. Mr. Campbell's voice drones on and on like a mosquito I wish I could swat. I keep looking at the clock and wondering where Mom and Denise are. Stopped at a gas station for a snack? Checking in at Hopestead? Meeting with the nursing staff? A note lands on my desk, folded into a neat little package. I open it up and see Benji's handwriting curling across the page.

Are you okay? You're twitchy.

I straighten up immediately and pretend to be fascinated in the lesson.

***

When we come home the house is quiet: no hair dryer, no country radio, no chatting. Denise won't be done work till five, so it's just me and Benji until then. It's too creepy downstairs with the Hair Emporium closed, so we stay in the kitchen to do our homework.

"It's weird," Benji says.

"What's weird?" I snap, even though I know exactly what he's referring to.

"The house, it's so quiet."

I shrug.

"I kind of like it," I lie.

I try not to think of Mom in a strange bed in a big house full of other cancer patients. Instead, I attack my math homework. I have never been so grateful for long division.

***

"I thought for our first night I'd make you something special for dinner." Denise says.

"I thought you hated cooking."

Denise frowns and plants her hands on her hips. "I never said that. When did I say that? Anyways, what do you feel like? Roast chicken? Meatloaf? Casserole?"

None of these sound delicious in any way.

"Can't we just order pizza?"

Denise pouts. "Well that's no fun. Pick something special."

Denise plucks a cookbook from on top of the fridge and plops it on the table in front of me. It's been there so long that the cover has a film of thick dust. Mom and I aren't into eating things that require written instructions. If it can't be boiled, Shake'n Baked or stir-fried, we don't bother. I draw a big C in the dust with my finger. When I was little I used to draw the letter C everywhere, in the gravel, in the snow, on the car window when it was all frosty in the morning. A big C for Clarissa. Now that C makes me think of cancer.

"Anything?" I ask.

"Anything," Denise promises.

I flip through the glossy pages, looking for something with little to no vegetables and lots of cheese. Or better yet, ribs. I love ribs.

"Can we have mussels?"

"I'm allergic to shellfish."

"Lamb?"

Denise is horrified. "What kind of a person eats baby sheep?" she asks.

"Fancy people," I say.

"Heartless people," Denise says.

"You eat cows and chickens," I point out.

"That's different."

"No, it's not. You said I could pick anything," I complain.

"Within reason," Denise adds.

"Well, then I want this." I open the book to something called beef bourguignon. The instructions go on for two pages.

"You're sure this is what you want?" Denise asks.

"I'm sure."

"Fine," Denise sighs. "I just have to pick up a few things from the grocery store."

She grabs a pencil and starts making a list. Some of the ingredients I've never heard of.

"Can Benji stay, too?" I ask.

"Sure thing, kiddo. The more the merrier."

***

Denise insists that she wants no help from us and shoos us out of the kitchen. Instead, we sit on the floor of my bedroom looking through Benji's comics and old magazines from the waiting area. Every once in awhile there is a big bang or a clatter as something falls to the ground. Denise swears under her breath, but not so quietly that we don't hear it from the bedroom. Then, after all that banging around, it's eerily silent. Benji looks concerned.

"Do you think we should see if she needs any help?" he asks.

"She said she wanted to do it herself," I remind him.

"I know, but it's been ages. I'm getting hungry."

"I don't think she's in the kitchen anymore. She's probably just waiting for it to cook."

I crawl toward the vent and press my ear to the slats. Sure

enough, I can just hear the sounds of the TV coming from the basement.

"What did I tell you? She's watching TV."

"Can we at least grab a snack?"

"Fine."

But snack time will have to wait, because when we get to the kitchen, the stove is on fire.

Burned

"Oh no, oh no, oh no, oh no . . ."

"Benji, snap out of it! Denise! *Denise!*"

Benji grabs a dish towel and waves it at the flames that crawl out from the burner and make their way across the pot. They reach so high the side of the cupboard is singed black.

"You're making it worse!"

I push him aside and make for the tap, filling a cereal bowl left over from breakfast with water.

"Move!"

I push past him again, water sloshing over the sides and getting all over my sleeves, but I don't even feel it. I can't feel anything but the heat from the fire. How can such a little fire make so much heat? Standing as close to the stove as I can while still feeling safe, I toss the water on the burner. My hands are shaking so badly I miss the pot and end up watering the floor instead. The smoke alarm kicks in and starts wailing away. Denise enters the kitchen and immediately starts swearing.

"Sweet Jesus! Kids, go to the living room — I'll deal with this."

Denise throws open the cupboards, shoving aside plates and cups.

"Where in God's name do you keep your baking soda?" she asks.

"In the fridge," I say.

"Well, don't just stand there, grab it!"

Denise puts on the oven mitts and throws our largest pot lid over the mess on the stove. Then she reaches around it to turn off the burner. I hand her the box of baking soda from the back of our fridge. After about a minute, she approaches the stove again.

"Stay back, kids," she says.

Carefully, she lifts the lids and pours the entire box of baking soda over the smouldering mess that was supposed to be our special dinner. At least the fire is out.

Denise takes a few deep breaths.

"Should we call the fire department?" I ask, breaking the silence.

"No," Denise says. "I've got it under control. What were you thinking, throwing water on a grease fire? You *never* throw water on a grease fire!"

"How am I supposed to know that?" I yell. "I was thinking that my house was going to burn down and I had to do something about it!"

Denise's face is almost as red as her hair, and I can tell she's not through yelling at me. But then she must remember that she's supposed to be the adult here, because she heaves a big sigh and shakes it off instead.

"Fine. I'm sorry. Benji, order a pizza. Clarissa, go get me your mother's biggest bottle of Annie-Off. And if I hear one word from your smart mouth, so help me God . . ."

But I don't say a single thing. Even though there are so many things I want to say, I keep them to myself. I want to live to see my mother's face when she comes home and finds her cupboards and a pan ruined, and sassing the woman who almost burned our house down is a sure way to get myself killed.

***

"My turn," Benji says. "Would you rather be Michelle Tanner's babysitter or be Kimmy Gibbler's best friend."

"I hate *Full House* questions."

Benji grins. "I know."

"Even though Kimmy Gibbler is annoying, she isn't as annoying as goody-goody Michelle Tanner, so if I had to, I'd be Kimmy Gibbler's best friend. My turn."

I'm going to have to get him good for that one.

"Would you rather eat Denise's cooking or eat raw sheep guts?"

Benji shudders. "Ugh, neither."

"You have to answer."

"Denise's cooking. At least it's not raw."

"You might as well lick the barbeque grill, it probably tastes the same."

Benji giggles. We're lying on my bed, staring at the glow-in-the-dark stars on the ceiling. I made my mom put them up two years ago when we were studying the solar system and they've been there ever since. They used to shine almost all night long, but now they last about twenty minutes before fading away to plain old ceiling white. I can't bring myself to take them down.

"Knock, knock."

I don't understand why Denise can't knock like a normal person. Instead she says the words "knock, knock" and walks right on in before you can say "go away."

"It's time for Benji to go," Denise says.

I sit up on my elbows and look over at the clock.

"But it's not even nine," I point out.

"It's a school night." Denise says.

"So?"

"So you two need your beauty sleep."

"But I'm not tired yet. I never fall asleep before eleven."

I use my best sappy Michelle Tanner eyes. If Mom was here she would have sent Benji home earlier, but Denise doesn't need to know that. For a second it looks like she's going to fall for it, but something comes over her and she shakes her head.

"Not tonight," she insists.

"I'd feel safer if he stayed," I say. "What if there's another fire?"

Denise's eyes narrow and she crosses her arms over her chest.

"Benji, Clarissa will see you tomorrow."

Benji hops off the bed, gathers his backpack and coat and smiles at Denise as he leaves. "Okay. Thanks for the pizza, Denise. Bye, Clarissa."

"Bye."

After he leaves, Denise and I stare at each other.

"Well, I'm going to watch TV and then I'll make my bed up in the living room," she says. "If you need anything, you know where I am."

She turns to leave and then looks back at me over her shoulder.

"Good night," she says stiffly.

"Good night," I answer.

It feels weird. I can't remember the last time Mom and I said good night; usually we just sort of wander off after dinner to do our own thing. I wonder what she's doing this very minute, and if anyone said good night to her.

Book

I can't sleep. I've been trying for hours. No matter what I do I can't seem to get comfortable. Denise is snoring away in the living room. She sounds like a lawn mower. No wonder I can't sleep. I punch my pillows into shape, throw off my duvet, pull it back up again, but nothing works. Instead I decide to I read.

I'm not really a big reader. I like reading fine; I just don't spend all day and all night with my nose in a book like some people do. My favourite books are the Wizard of Oz books. I have read all fourteen books in the series, some of them more than once, like *Ozma of Oz*, which I might like even more than *The Wonderful Wizard of Oz*.

I inherited all of my Oz books from Mom, which she had when she was little. They have delicate paper covers with old-fashioned paintings of a girl with blond curls and a short dress. She looks nothing like Dorothy in the movie. Apparently when Mom was my age she loved The Wizard of Oz, too. It's hard to imagine her reading anything other than a magazine, let alone something as magical as The Wizard of Oz. She's not really the fantasy type, but she read me the first Oz book and I've been hooked ever since. The others I read on my own, but I remember how exciting it was when she'd come into my room before bed and read me one chapter a night.

Now I'm reading them all over again. They are just as good as I remembered. I read until my eyes are so heavy that I have no choice but to fall asleep. It seems to be the only thing that works.

***

"I bought you some things for lunch," Denise says.

I look through the grocery bags and find a big jar of peanut butter.

"I can't eat this," I say, putting it back in the bag.

"When did you get so picky?" Denise complains.

"I can't bring peanut butter. I'm not allowed."

"Not allowed?"

"Because of nut allergies," I explain.

"You've got to be kidding me."

"Sorry."

"When I was in school no one was allergic to peanuts," Denise says.

I snort. "Was peanut butter even invented back then?"

"Fine, smarty pants. You can have bread and water then."

Figures. That's what they serve criminals in prisons, isn't it?

Branded

The first time I see the flyer, I don't think anything of it. There are just some kids huddled around a piece of paper laughing. But then I see other people in the halls with the same orange flyer, and by lunchtime it seems like everyone has one. Everyone except me and Benji. I don't like to be left out of a joke, especially a big school-wide thing, so I march up to Mattie and ask to see her flyer. She won't look me in the eye.

"Flyer?" she says sweetly.

"Yeah, the orange thing you stuffed in your pocket. Can I see it?"

"Why?" Mattie asks.

"Because I lost mine," I lie.

"It's nothing you want to see," Mattie says.

"Oh never mind."

I stomp off in search of another flyer, but they are maddeningly hard to find. That is until the bell rings and we head inside and find Benji's locker covered in orange flyers. I rip one down to get a closer look. Someone has photocopied the definition of homosexual and pasted Benji's yearbook photo underneath.

I try to shove Benji out of the way so he doesn't see them, but there are too many. Whoever it was — and I have a pretty good idea who's behind it — has used packing tape, which makes it extremely hard to peel the flyers off. A group of people are pointing at us, me tearing at Benji's locker and Benji just staring there all white-faced.

"What are you looking at?" I yell. They don't even look guilty. I really hate people sometimes.

Suddenly Michael Greenblat is there, passing me a mini Swiss Army knife. "Here, use this."

He looks nervous, maybe because he doesn't want to be seen helping us out, or maybe because he knows pocket knives are not allowed at school and he doesn't want to be caught. I slip the knife out of his hand and slice through the packing tape.

"Thanks," I say, but when I turn to give it back Michael is already slinking away.

"Keep it," he mutters. "I have another one."

What am I supposed to do with a knife? I pocket it and hope that I don't get caught with it.

The warning bell goes and I hurry to stuff the flyers in the garbage can, but not before folding one up and putting it in my binder. Benji looks sick.

"We need one for evidence," I explain, but he doesn't look convinced.

"I don't feel well," he mumbles.

I don't know what to say. I can't find the words to make Terry or the orange flyers or the whole thing go away. Instead I walk with him to class with my head up, daring anyone to say anything.

***

Benji goes home straight after school, claiming he feels sick to his stomach. I call him a few times but no one picks up.

Denise won't be home till later, not that I'd tell her any of this stuff. She'd probably just overreact and call the police, although maybe that wouldn't be such a bad idea. I can't talk to Mom about it because she already thinks I went to the teacher and she'd be mad as a hatter when she found out I lied. Mr. Campbell is out of the question, and none of the kids at school care enough to do anything either. They've never really given Benji a chance.

And so I decide to write another letter to Principal Donner. This time I tell her that Mr. Campbell is "not the sharpest tool in the kit," and that he misses things that happen right before his own eyes. At least that's half true. By the time I've printed and signed it, I'm starting to feel a bit better.

I take the Swiss Army knife out of my pocket and hide it at the back of my sock drawer, next to the geode Michael gave me. For a second I think about calling him but I don't know what I'd say. Why did you help me this afternoon? Thanks for the rock and the knife? No, I can't call him. It would be too weird. Besides I don't even have his number. I don't understand boys. Still, it's nice to get gifts, even if they are rocks and knives.

***

For some reason Denise thinks it is important for us to eat dinner together every night. She doesn't make the mistake of trying her luck in the kitchen again, but sticks to the things she knows: pasta, takeout and frozen dinners. She pours a glass of wine for herself and lets me have a can of root beer, even though my mother would kill her if she knew. Some rules she sticks to like glue, but others she breaks without even batting a false eyelash.

"We almost never eat in the kitchen," I say. "You know that. You've been here enough times."

"I just thought it would be nice," Denise says. "So. Any cute boys in your class or have you got your sights set on an older man? Maybe someone in grade eight? What about that boy with the rock? What was his name again?"

"His name is Michael, and it's a geode, and I don't like him."

"Okay, okay. Just trying to make a little friendly conversation."

We go back to eating our Lean Cuisine chicken pot pies in silence for awhile.

"You know, when your mother was younger, she had men falling all over her, too. And just like you, she didn't give them the time of day. I guess the apple doesn't fall far from the tree."

I look up but Denise is digging into her dinner like she hasn't eaten in a week.

"Really?"

Denise nods. "You bet. I was positively sick with envy. I would've given anything for just one of those boys to look my way. Sometimes it was hard to be best friends with Annie Delaney."

I don't know why Denise is telling me this. It makes me feel uncomfortable. But a small part of me knows exactly how she feels, the part of me that thinks that sometimes it's hard to be Annie Delaney's daughter. Not that I'd ever tell her that.

***

Every night around eight o'clock my stomach starts to hurt. Nothing serious, just a little ache, like when you eat too much ice cream or are about to write a big test. It hurts right up until the phone rings and I hear my mother's voice and then I can go back to feeling normal again. We always have the same conversation.

"Hi, baby. How was school?"

"Fine."

"Anything funny happen?"

"Not really."

"How's Benji?"

"Fine," I lie.

"Are you being good for Denise?"

Am I being *good for Denise*? Like I'm some sort of little kid and Denise is my babysitter.

"Yes."

This is the part where I'm supposed to ask her how she's feeling, but I can't bring myself to do it. If I were a better person maybe I could, but the truth is I don't want to know. If I ask her how she's feeling and the answer is bad, then I have to think about how maybe she won't get better. Or that even if she gets better this time, cancer can always come back.

"Good. It makes me happy to know you two are getting along together."

I didn't exactly say that, but I let it slide. I don't want her to worry about anything except getting better. What she doesn't know can't hurt her. She tells me funny stories about the people she lives with and they all seem so normal that I forget that she's away getting cancer treatment. I imagine that she's at a big stylist's convention, learning about new products and trading hair secrets.

"Well, put Denise on and I'll let you get back to your homework."

"Okay. Bye."

"Bye, baby. I miss you."

"I miss you, too."

At least that much is true.

122

Bathrooms

Disaster strikes during history.

"Mr. Campbell, may I have the washroom pass, please?"

He barely looks up at me from the overhead on ancient Egypt. "You just got back from lunch, Clarissa."

"Yes."

"Lunch or recess is the preferred time to use the washroom."

"I know."

"If you go now, you will miss out on the thrilling secret of Tutankhamen's tomb."

"Isn't it in the textbook?"

Mr. Campbell throws his hands in the air. "Clarissa, Clarissa! Where is your sense of adventure? Of course it's in the textbook, but I am going to reveal it to you piece by piece, as a sort of riddle. The Egyptians were crazy about riddles."

I don't care for riddles. They've been ruined by teachers who use them to teach you something and take all the fun out of them.

"I really need to go," I insist.

Mr. Campbell sighs and gestures at the pass, hanging on a nail by the door. "Far be it for me to stand in the way of nature," he says.

I slide out of my desk and saunter to the doorway as if nothing is out of the ordinary. I even take the time to shut the door gently behind me, which is more than I do in my own house. After I'm out of sight of the classroom, I walk as fast as I can without looking too stupid to the girl's bathroom.

There in the stall my worst fears come true. I hadn't been imagining things in class. There is a spot on my underwear. A brownish red spot. At first I'm not sure what it is. I thought it would be more red. How can this be? I am as flat as flat can be and yet here I am, with a dark stain staring up at me from the inside of my underwear. You are supposed to develop first and *then* get your period. That's what the video said in health class. Everything is backward.

I check my jeans and hallelujah, there's no stain; it hadn't leaked through my underwear. I ball up a wad of toilet paper and start dabbing at the stain, but then I remember the time when Denise spilled red wine on my mom's good (well, only) tablecloth, and Mom told her not to wipe at it because it would rub it in and she'd never be able to get it out. What if blood is like wine, and I am ruining my underwear forever? Not that it matters. The second I get home I'm going to throw them out so no one will ever find them. If I ever get out of the bathroom, that is.

How long have I been sitting here? Two minutes? Ten? Sooner or later Mr. Campbell will notice that I'm not back yet. He'll send someone to come check on me. Then what? I could say I was sick, that I had bad ham in my sandwich and now I'm throwing up all over the place. I could blame Denise, who isn't used to making lunches, and say she must have forgotten to check the expiry date before piling on the meat. All it would take is for Mr. Campbell to look in our fridge and he'd believe it in a second.

But even if I do make it back to class, how can I possibly act like everything is normal? I feel like a preschooler who has wet her pants, except this is way worse. When you're a little kid no one cares if you wet your pants. Everyone has accidents once in awhile and everyone forgets about them the next day. People even bring spare underpants with them. But this is different. This, I'm supposed to be prepared for. Seventh graders are mean. And they never forget. I'll never live it down.

And then there's the problem of further stain prevention. There is a dispenser on the wall of the bathroom, but how am I supposed to get there with my underwear around my knees? Whoever designs bathrooms should really put a dispenser inside every stall. I hate this stupid bathroom in this stupid school. I hate being a girl. It's not fair. Nothing happens to boys.

Now I'm actually starting to feel sick. My lunch is starting to bubble in my stomach and I've got that sour taste in my mouth that usually means I'm about to throw up. It's getting harder to swallow the lumps in my throat, but I will not allow myself to cry.

Just then the door swings open and a pair of fussy black shoes with straps and ladybug buckles appears. You don't need to be a genius at Whose Shoes to guess who it is. Only one person would wear ridiculous shoes like that.

"Clarissa?" says Mattie.

I resist the urge to draw my feet up onto the toilet seat. What good would it do? She already knows I'm here. There is only one girls' bathroom on the second floor and she probably saw my feet when she walked in.

"Clarissa, are you okay?"

The last person I want to talk to is Mattie Cohen. She

125

probably volunteered to come and check on me. What a
suck-up. This has to be the universe punishing me for being
such a bad daughter.

"Clarissa?" She knocks on the stall. "I know you're in
there. Are you sick?"

"No. Well. Sort of."

I watch as Mattie's feet take a big step back from the stall.
"Did you throw up?"

"No."

There's a long pause. I begin to hope that she's left, but
then her feet reappear by the stall.

"Is it — I mean, do you need, like, something from the
dispenser?"

This is my chance. I can sit here until school gets out and
hope no one else comes looking for me, which is unlikely,
or ask Mattie Cohen to get me a pad. I know what the right
choice is but that doesn't make it any easier. Mattie can't
keep a secret. In ten minutes the whole class will know that
Clarissa Delaney has her period. But what other option do
I have?

"Yes." There. I said it. The jig is up.

"I'll get you one! My mom gave me an emergency quar-
ter for this sort of thing but I've never had to use it. I haven't
gotten mine yet. You're so lucky, Clarissa."

I don't feel lucky. I feel heavy. Plus, my stomach is really
starting to ache. Maybe these are my first cramps. On the
other side of the stall, Mattie kneels and passes me a pad
wrapped up in a light pink wrapper.

"What does it feel like?" she asks.

"Wet."

"Ewww, that's gross."

"Of course, it's gross. It's blood."

The pad is huge, like someone cut a fat strip out of a diaper. I stand up. It even feels like I'm wearing a diaper. Will people be able to tell? Oh, well. It's either ruin my clothing or wear the diaper — or worse, a tampon, and I don't even want to think about that process. I flush the toilet and emerge from the stall, almost smacking Mattie in the face with the door.

"Cripes, do you have to stand so *close?*"

Mattie jumps back and looks me up and down, like she's searching for proof.

"Do you feel different?" she asks.

"Not really. My stomach hurts a little."

Mattie nods. "Cramps. My mother says the best thing to do is to lie in bed with a hot water bottle and avoid sugar."

I'm pretty sure we don't have a water bottle. Maybe I can convince Mom to get me one. Then the realization hits me like a sucker punch to the stomach. Mom's not home. I'll have to tell Denise. She'll probably cry and insist on doing my makeup to welcome me to womanhood. Barf. If only there was a way to keep it secret from her, but someone needs to go to the drugstore and buy me my own supply of pads, and I don't think I can stand any more embarrassment.

"My mom gave me this book and it said that once you get your period, you are no longer a girl, but a real woman, like a caterpillar turning into a butterfly."

"That is the dumbest thing I've ever heard. Butterflies don't bleed."

Mattie looks disappointed. "So you don't feel any different at all?"

"No."

That isn't exactly true. I don't feel any different, but I know that from now on things have changed. I wonder how old my mother was when she got her period, and if she got

127

cramps. I wonder how long her period is, and if I should expect mine to be the same. What brand of (ugh) pad does she use? There are lots of things I want to ask her, but she is scheduled for another round of chemo this afternoon. It will have to wait. I wash my hands with extra soap and then I wash them again. Mattie is staring at me in the mirror.

"Are the cramps really bad?" she asks.

"Yes," I lie.

"Maybe you can go home. I'll go with you to the nurse."

"Okay." My voice wobbles dangerously. Tears are building up again behind my eyes. I just want to be home and away from everyone and everything. I don't feel like a woman at all. I feel like a baby. What is wrong with me? I yank my shirt down as far as it will go and frown into the mirror.

"Don't worry," Mattie says. "You can't tell at all."

I don't know how she does it, but Mattie sure is good at reading people's minds.

"Not even when I walk?" I ask.

I head toward the door, sure that I'm walking as bowlegged as a cowboy in a cartoon. But Mattie shakes her head.

"No, you just look like regular Clarissa."

"Good."

Mattie marches right into the nurse's office and announces that I'm feeling very under the weather and need to go home. I keep my mouth shut and let her do most of the talking. When the nurse asks me what my symptoms are, Mattie cuts in and says, "I found her in the bathroom throwing up," without blinking an eye. The nurse has me lay down on a cot with a cloth over my eyes. She sends Mattie to get my things while she calls home.

"I'll just give your mother a call and tell her to come pick you up," she says.

"My mother's in London," I say. And because I'm feeling mean, I add, "She's at Hopestead Manor, recovering from cancer treatment. You have to call Denise Renzetti."

There is a silence and the rustling of paper and I know the nurse is checking my file. How can she not know about my situation? Everyone else seems to know about it. The nurse clears her throat and I know she feels bad about mentioning my mother. She should feel bad! I wonder if she could be fired for making such a stupid mistake.

"Ah, here it is. Denise Renzetti."

My stomach is really hurting now, and the pain has spread to my lower back. I can't hold back the tears any longer. They slip silently from under my lashes and soak into the cloth over my eyes. Thank goodness for that cloth. I guess the universe or someone has started to feel sorry for me. About time.

***

In the car I say nothing to Denise and she asks me no questions. I overheard the nurse telling her that there is a flu going around and I seem to have caught it. Some nurse. She didn't even take my temperature. I could have something really terrible, but she took Mattie's word. It just goes to show you that goody-two-shoes teacher's pets like Mattie Cohen can get away with anything.

Denise buys it hook, line and sinker. "I'm sorry I can't stay with you, Clarissa, but I've got a real big client at two. Is there something you want me to bring back for you from the grocery store? Ginger ale? Chicken soup?"

I shrug and stare out the window at all the people going about their normal lives. It always surprises me to see how many people there are walking around, not in school or at work, and not just moms and babies. Teenagers, adults, all sorts of people. I wonder how many of them are playing hooky, like me, or how many of them have their periods.

Denise sighs and I can tell she's trying real hard to be understanding, even though she hates it when I pull a Sullen Sally. The truth is I don't think I can bring myself to ask for what I really need. I decide to check under the sink first. Denise pulls into the driveway.

"Ginger ale would be good," I mutter.

"Ginger ale it is. See you in a few hours."

***

It's quiet in the house, except for the hum of the refrigerator and every once in awhile the rattle of hot air rushing through the vents. It makes me feel cozy. The first thing I do is root out a bag of chips and two s'mores granola bars. Then I turn the radio on loud enough to hear it in the bathroom, where I run a bath as hot as I can stand it. I use a double dose of bubble bath and soon the bubbles are so thick and frothy I can't see the water below them, like extra thick vanilla icing on a birthday cake.

I peel off my clothes and throw them in the hamper, except for the ruined underwear, which I wrap in the empty chip bag and shove way down in the garbage can where I can be sure it will never be found. It's almost like it never happened. Then I sink beneath the bubbles and let them work their cleaning, tingling magic. The man on the radio is giving away $10,000 to the next caller and I think about what I would do with that money. Go on a trip, maybe. With Mom, Benji, and maybe Denise, if I'm feeling extra nice. Maybe we could go to Disneyland.

After my bath I feel warm and sleepy. It's just after three

o'clock in the afternoon. School's out and Denise will be home with my ginger ale soon. All I want to do is curl up in bed and sleep away the next five to seven days, but first I need to be sure that nothing like today's incident ever happens again. Sure enough, under the sink I find a whole stash of pads. With wings, without, long, contoured, pantiliners. Who knew there were so many types? The idea of leakage makes my heart beat faster, so I go for extra long with wings. The more protection the better. This one doesn't feel as bulky as the pad from the girl's bathroom, but I can still feel it. I wonder if I'll ever get used to it.

Once I'm in bed the phone rings. It's Benji, I know it is. It's something I've always been able to do, like those people on TV who say they knew that the phone call was bad news before they even answered it. A sort of ESP thing — not that I believe in that kind of hocus-pocus, but there isn't any other way to explain it. I guess some people are more connected than others.

I let the phone ring, four times, five, until I lose count. I don't feel like talking to him. I don't want to tell him about the bathroom, or Mattie, or any of it. He wouldn't understand. He's a boy, how could he? Of all the bad things about the whole situation, not being able to tell Benji is one of the worst. Before this, I could tell him anything and he would understand. I never thought there would be a day when I didn't want to tell him something about my life. Especially something so huge. This was something we couldn't share, ever. It makes the ache in my stomach worse.

The answering machine beeps and whoever it is doesn't leave a message, which just proves it was Benji because answering machines make him nervous and he never leaves a message.

Bluff

"Clarissa? It's for you."

I must have fallen asleep, because suddenly Denise is at the door holding the phone. I blink and sit up quickly. My stomach hurts and I remember what I'm doing here, home, asleep in the middle of the afternoon, although now it's pretty dark outside. The alarm clock says it's ten past six. I can't believe I've slept that long. The cramps are pretty terrible, although the ache in my stomach might also have something to do with the two granola bars and bag of chips I ate earlier. I rub the sleep from my eyes and shake my head to wake up a little.

"Hello?" I say, yawning into the phone.

"Hi, Clarissa, it's Mattie."

I'm wide awake now. I was expecting to hear Benji's voice.

"Oh. Mattie. Hi."

"How are you feeling?"

Mattie's voice is so loud I'm sure Denise can hear it from the doorway, where she's standing, frowning at me, like she's trying to figure out what to do with a sick child. I turn away from her, toward the window.

"Okay," I mumble. "My head hurts a little."

"Are the cramps bad?" she asks, practically yelling into

the phone. Mattie never could take a hint. I'm afraid to look at Denise, in case she heard.

"They're okay. Like I said, it's my *head* that hurts. Everything's just so *loud*."

Mattie is skeptical. "I've never heard of that symptom before," she says.

"Well, you wouldn't know, would you?"

The words are out of my mouth before I can stop them.

"I mean, you're not the one with the — well, you know. But you will know, someday. Sorry."

"It's okay," says Mattie. "Mood swings are very common during the menstrual period."

"Oh, right." I clench my teeth to keep anything else from flying out of my mouth.

"Do you have any questions about the homework?" Mattie asks brightly.

"What homework?" I ask.

"Benji said he was going to bring over your homework," Mattie says. She's getting that bossy tone in her voice, the one she gets when someone hasn't lived up to the Mattie Cohen standard. It makes me want to defend him.

"I was asleep all afternoon, so maybe he did come by and I didn't hear the bell," I say.

"Oh. Well, if you have any questions or if he doesn't bring it over by eight, call me and I'll go over it with you."

"Okay. Thanks," I say. I try to sound enthusiastic, even though there is no way I will call her to do homework over the phone.

"Oh, don't thank me, it's the least I can do," says Mattie. She sounds very pleased with herself. "Now you should get back to bed! Are you using the hot water bottle?"

Cripes, that Mattie is bossy.

"Yes," I lie. "It's great!"

I can practically hear her beaming through the telephone.

"I told you! See you tomorrow, Clarissa."

"Bye Mattie."

When I hang up and roll over, Denise is still in the doorway. Except now she's holding the open box of extra-long Kotex with wings. I must have left it on the floor of the bathroom. I feel my cheeks getting hot and I burrow further into the blankets. Maybe if I play sick she'll go away. She doesn't.

"What's this? Is this why you came home from school today?" she asks, shaking the Kotex box.

I nod, burrowing a little further into the blankets.

"And my stomach hurt," I add.

"Why didn't you—" but Denise stops mid-sentence. I know what she was about to say. Why didn't I tell her the truth? And it's because I didn't want to talk to her. She shouldn't be the one here right now. I look down at the bed and pick at the hairy tufts of the bedspread. When I was little I thought they looked like fat pink caterpillars. That seems like a long time ago. Denise lets out a big sigh and perches at the end of my bed.

"God, I wish your mother was here," she says.

"Me, too."

Denise looks at me like maybe she wants to hug me but we've never really been huggy-huggy, Denise and I. Instead, she heaves one of her famous world-weary sighs and stares at the Kotex box in her hands.

"Do you have any questions?" she mumbles.

I can't believe it. For once in her life she doesn't know what to say. I think about what a miracle this is, and if only Benji were here to see it. Then I remember that everything is different now, and where would I even start to tell him all this? It's probably better he doesn't know. He can be very queasy.

I shrug.

"We pretty much covered it in health," I say. Which is partly true. Last year they sent all the girls to the art room to watch videos and draw diagrams of unspeakably embarrassing body parts. In none of the videos did it talk about what a cramp would feel like, or say that the blood can be more brownish than red, or mention that it's not just your stomach but sometimes your whole body that kind of aches.

"You know, when I was your age I didn't have sex ed or women's health or whatever the schools are calling it now. They pretty much sat us down and told us if we French-kissed a boy we would get pregnant."

I am absolutely certain this is not the sort of birds and bees talk my mother would approve of. Denise seems to think so, too, because she keeps twiddling her ring round her finger and jiggling her foot.

"I'm sure your mother would put it better than me," she says. Then something happens and Denise snaps out of her jittery mode and gets a glint in her eye.

"Hey, why don't we ask her?" she says.

I sit up.

"You mean call her?"

Denise jumps up and starts pacing the room, a big horsey smile spreading over her face.

"Better. Do you have any tests tomorrow? Anything important?" she asks.

"No."

"Do you think you feel up to a little road trip?"

My heart leaps.

"You mean skip school?"

"One little day won't hurt you. Lord knows I skipped my fair share of classes and I turned out all right."

I open my mouth to say otherwise but Denise holds up her hand and stops me.

"Try to restrain yourself, Clarissa. I know it's difficult, but I'm doing something nice for you."

"It's kind of for you, too." I point out.

"Well, yes it is, but it's still a damn nice thing to do. So pack your bag, kiddo. We're going to see your mama."

Breakaway

In half an hour I am packed and sitting in the front seat of Denise's car, clutching a pillow on my lap and grinning from ear to ear. Denise is running around the house making last minute calls and looking for her toothbrush. My insides are so jittery I don't think I can stand just sitting here in the driveway much longer. How long does it take to find a toothbrush? I lean on the horn. Finally the lights in the house go out and Denise comes running down the stairs, huffing and puffing, coat open and flapping around her.

She opens the back door and throws her bags in the back. "I'm coming, Clarissa — keep your pants on."

She slides into the driver's seat. "Here, take my purse," she says between big gasps of air.

"You really should quit smoking," I say.

"Don't. Push. It," she wheezes, but she's smiling like nothing can put her in a bad mood. "If you open the inside pocket you'll find a pack of gum," she says. "Do me a favour and get me a piece, will you? You take one, too."

"But it's Nicorette gum," I say.

"Darn, I thought I had the real stuff in there. Sorry, kiddo, there might be a mint or something for you."

There isn't. But I don't mind. In ninety minutes I will be seeing my mother.

In all the excitement I never got a chance to call Benji, but as we pull out of the driveway I see the curtains in his front window move. Guilt gnaws at my stomach when I remember how I left school suddenly, never called him to explain, and am now making a secret getaway in the night with one of my least favourite people. But sometimes a girl's gotta do what a girl's gotta do. I know he'll understand.

**

Denise is a lot more fun in the car than I thought she would be. First of all, unlike my mother, Denise thinks country music is for old folks and rednecks. "And we, Clarissa, are not rednecks. And, despite what you may think, I am not all that old, either." This means we get to listen to the top eight at eight on the regular radio station. Denise knows all the words to every song, and I'm in such a good mood it doesn't even bother me when she sings along. Soon, I'm singing along at the top of my lungs and I don't care what I look like or who can hear me, because it feels great.

"Sing it, girl," Denise yells, and she opens the window so I can shout out the song as we fly down the highway into the dark, endless night. The cool wind whips the hair around my face and I feel like we're in a movie. I haven't felt this good in a long time.

**

We make one stop along the way at a gas station. Denise gives the attendant a twenty and tells him to "Fill 'er up." Then she winks at him, even though he is young enough to be her son. I roll my eyes but I am in too good a mood to say anything else, especially when Denise gives me $10 and tells me to pick out some provisions.

Besides the woman behind the cash, who doesn't even look up when I enter, I am the only one in the store. The lights are so bright they hurt my eyes. I scan the shelves for Delaney standards, like Miss Vickie's chips, peanut M&M's and Rainbow Twizzlers. I think about getting a 2-litre bottle of Coke but decide that ginger ale is better for Mom, who is probably feeling sick from the chemo. With my arms full of goodies, I saunter up to the cash register.

"Going on a diet?" the cashier asks. She laughs at her own joke, her enormous bosom shaking under her ketchup-red and mustard-yellow gas-station uniform shirt. Her hair is brassy yellow with dark roots and is so full of gel it looks like she just got out of the shower. I resist the urge to snort.

When I don't answer, she asks me, "Going on a road trip?"

I shrug like it's no big deal or maybe none of her business, which it isn't.

"Maybe."

"Well, have a good time."

And because I am in such a good mood, I leave a whole toonie in the tip cup, just to show her what a good person I am and how I am above the likes of her. Besides, it's Denise's money.

***

When we reach London my stomach seizes up with excitement, or maybe it's nerves. I can't tell which. Denise unfolds the map and spreads it out over the steering wheel. She taps it with a finger and reads the street names aloud to herself.

"Hoyle. Dunmore—"

"Did you call and tell her we were coming?" I ask.

"Nope," Denise says. "I can't wait to see the look on her face. But don't worry, I called the nurse, and she says she's doing good today. She'll be happy to have some surprise visitors. Wellington. Ah, Wellington. Here we are."

Hopestead House is smaller than I expected. It looks like any old house, neat and tidy, painted white with blue shutters. The curtains are all shut, but they're ruffled along the edges, like old-fashioned skirts, with light sneaking out from underneath like petticoats. There's even a wraparound porch with a wicker loveseat out front. Inside a place like this you'd expect to see a mom baking cookies, or an old lady knitting in a rocking chair, not a lot of cancer patients with needles sticking out of their arms. My stomach clenches like a fist; will there be needles in Mom's arm?

I step out of the car and wait for Denise to grab her bags.

"Ready, kiddo?"

We walk up the neat little stairs, past the flower boxes, and in through the front door. One of those embroidered pillows hangs in the window, white with blue stitching. A *Stranger is a Friend You Haven't Met*, it says, surrounded by a whole lot of little blue flowers. They have five points, like stars. Maybe one of the cancer patients made it. Maybe they have someone come in and teach them how to embroider while they recover. But I can't imagine Mom sitting in a circle, gabbing away, stitching a welcome sign or a pillow, though. She's not what you'd call a crafty sort of person.

"Hello?"

Denise and I stand in the front foyer, looking around for signs of life. The only thing that makes Hopestead different from a regular house is the desk set up just under the stairs. There isn't a receptionist in sight, but a little sign that says "Back in 5" sits on top of a pile of paperwork. Somewhere in the house a TV is on; I can hear the rise and fall of the laugh track of some stupid sitcom, but it isn't loud enough to tell what sitcom it is.

"Clarissa?"

And suddenly she's there: wrapped in her old purple bathrobe, the one that's worn out in places, like the elbows on an old teddy bear, standing at the top of the stairs. I am relieved that, even though her hair is pulled back and I can tell from here it's greasier than usual, she still looks like Mom. In my head, I have been picturing her as one of those concentration camp survivors from the videos we watched in history: thin, grey and bald. I'm surprised to find I've been holding my breath. I let it out.

"Surprise," I manage to say, but the word wobbles in my throat. Holding tight to the banister I take the stairs two at a time until I'm right in front of her. Mom smoothes the hair from my forehead and steadies my chin in her hand.

"Come on, I'll show you my room."

I manage to hold it in until we get to Mom's bedroom. Once we're safe inside I press my face into her bathrobe and let it all out. Feeling Mom's hands running through my hair and tickling my neck just makes it worse. I sob and sob until my nose is runny and the front of her robe is damp with my tears. Finally the tears stop coming but my body still shudders, like it has more crying to do. The skin on my cheeks feels tight where my tears have dried.

"Better?" Mom asks.

I nod.

"Good."

When I pull away I see that she's been crying, too. Her skin looks grey and pulled tight, especially under her eyes.

"You don't look good," I say.

She laughs.

"Well, I'm not exactly at the spa," she says.

"Is it bad, Annie?"

I'm surprised to hear Denise. She must have come in right behind me, but I was too busy crying like a baby to notice. She's sitting in the rocker across from the bed, hands folded primly in her lap, like an old lady. She looks tired, too. Maybe she's been tired for awhile and I never noticed.

"Sometimes," Mom says. "But not always. It's better when you have visitors." She gives my shoulders a squeeze.

"We brought you something," I say.

I wiggle out of her arms and reach for the night bag at Denise's feet. For a moment I can't find the movie, and I think I might cry all over again. But no, there it is. I hold up *My Best Friend's Wedding* and smile triumphantly. Mom claps her hands and smiles widely.

"Good choice!" she says.

"We thought you might need it," Denise says.

"To tell you the truth, I've had a grade-A, red-alarm Julia Roberts kind of day," Mom says.

Denise snorts. "Join the club."

***

There's enough room in the bed for all three of us. I curl in next to Mom with my head close to her shoulder. She runs her hands through my hair like she used to when I was little and occasionally rests her chin on the top of my head. Denise sits near the end of the bed and attacks my mother's toes with a new nail polish called Winter Berry. Her pink tackle kit sits open beside her like a big sprawling octopus.

"Your nail beds look like the trenches, Annie," she says. "I'm leaving you a good moisturizer and some aloe socks."

I had forgotten that chemo does bad things to your

stomach, so Denise and I divide the gas station provisions between ourselves. I eat string after string of Rainbow Twizzlers, the ones Benji says taste like soap but that I just can't get enough of. Mom sips ginger ale from a paper cup and sucks on all-natural honey and lemon candies.

As comfortable as I am, I keep twisting around so I can sneak glances at Mom. Even though she's only been gone a week it feels like forever. It's nice to turn around and see her sitting right behind me. But you can only twist around to stare at someone so many times before they start to notice.

"What are you looking at?" Mom asks.

Well, now that she's brought it up, there is one thing I've been wondering about, but I don't want to ruin this moment. It feels normal, me, Mom, Denise and Julia Roberts.

"I was just thinking . . ." I start.

Mom raises an eyebrow and waits for me to continue. Sometimes there is no other way around something; you just have to say it.

"You still have your hair," I say.

Mom shifts and I sit up, not wanting to hurt her.

"Yes," she says. "I do, for now."

That "for now" hangs in the air like a thundercloud waiting to ruin everything. Mom loosens her ponytail and fluffs out her hair. It's then I see that it's not just greasier than normal, but it's thinner, too. I am alarmed at the amount of hair that clings to the elastic. Mom runs her fingers through her hair, raking out even more strands, and inspects the ends.

"I'm thinking of cutting it short," she says.

"Oh, Annie," Denise says and suddenly she's crying. "Oh, Annie, your hair!" she sobs.

I don't know where to look or what to do. I feel sad and uncomfortable and a little like laughing all at the same time. Just like everything else she does, Denise makes a big production out of crying — hiccupping and shaking and howling away like a dog. I'm sure they can hear her all over Hopestead House. Although I guess I should be thankful we're not outside or at the mall or something.

Denise keeps saying, "Your hair, your hair," over and over again. It's starting to get on my nerves. For someone who is supposed to be my mother's best friend she isn't being very considerate. It's not like *her* hair is going to fall out. How does she think Mom feels, hearing someone go to pieces over something that isn't even happening to her?

"*Shhh*," my mother says. "DeeDee, it's going to be all right. It's just hair; it'll grow back. That's what hair does."

"B–but you're a *stylist*, Annie!"

Mum shrugs. "So, I'll be a bald stylist. Maybe I can get a job at Curl Up & Dye."

Denise laughs wildly for a second, but then her face crumples and she's at it again. Mom rubs her arm.

"DeeDee, it's not forever."

Denise blows her nose into her sleeve and wipes her wet eyes with the back of her hand. Disgusting.

"I know," she says. "I know. I'm sorry."

As Mom shushes Denise, I think about Benji's essay and how he was right. Even when things are bad, Mom helps other people. She's the one with the cancer, but somehow she ends up being the strong one who makes other people feel better. Remembering the essay I feel ugly and ashamed that I didn't think of it first. How can I be so blind? What else have I gotten totally and completely wrong?

Breakfast

We three are so tuckered out from crying that we fall asleep before the movie's over. I awake with a start the next morning and find Denise snoring away beside me. I can't remember the last time I slept so soundly. My arm is stuck under her pillow. Carefully, so as not to wake her, I pull it out and shake away the pins and needles. Static buzzes on the TV screen. It reminds me of the mornings Mom would get me up and say, "Quick, Clarissa, come look! The weather station says it's going to be a snowstorm!" I would rush downstairs and see the static on the TV and then hear Mom laughing away upstairs. Just another example of a bad Mom joke, the kind I've been missing with her gone.

I let my eyes adjust to the semi-darkness and take a good look at the room. Mom has a corner room on the second floor. It has windows on two sides and a big iron bed covered in quilts, which squeaks when you climb into it. A low bookshelf is crammed under one window and full of books with titles like *I am Not my Breast Cancer*, *Breast Cancer: A Survivor's Guide* and *Real Women Talk about Cancer*. There is also a bible and a stack of fat romance novels.

On the nightstand, next to a glass of water, is a slim journal with a pen sticking out of the top like a bookmark.

"Good morning."

Mom yawns and sits up, rubbing at her eyes.

"What's that?" I ask.

"It's my journal," Mom says. "I read somewhere that it can be therapeutic to write down your feelings during the process."

I stare blankly at my mother. I have never known her to write down anything, not even a grocery list. Keeping track of your feelings sounds awfully granola to me. All of a sudden I notice that there are candles on almost every surface. Maybe they're those aromatherapy candles. In one week these Hopestead people have taken my mother and turned her into a granola hippie. Mom is running a finger up and down the spine of her new hippie journal. I hope she doesn't read it out loud, but at the same time, I wonder if she's written anything about me.

"Are you hungry?" she whispers.

I nod.

"Come on, let's go downstairs to the kitchen. I want you to meet everybody."

We slide out of bed as carefully as we can, not wanting to wake Denise, although I'm not sure that's even possible. She snorts once and rolls over, taking up the whole bed. Mom wraps herself up in her bathrobe and I throw on my fleece. Together we pad downstairs.

The kitchen at Hopestead is bright and sunny and surprisingly full this early in the morning. Two women sit across from each other, leaning over steaming mugs of tea. One of them has a nubby knitted cap pulled down to her ears. She's completely bald underneath. Her skin looks greyish, like clay, but she smiles and her eyes are friendly.

146

"This must be the famous Clarissa," she says. I'm surprised to hear that she has a British accent.

Mom puts her hands on my shoulders. "Morning everyone, this is my daughter Clarissa. The light of my life, or the highlights in my hair, as we say in hair business." I can't believe my mom would make a hair joke in front of the bald lady, but she laughs just as hard as anyone else.

"Lovely to meet you," she grasps my hand and shakes it. "I'm Joanne, and this is Carrie."

Carrie nods at me. She is all wrapped up in a bright scarf and wearing a kimono. She looks like an actress in a black and white movie, except for the bruises on the inside of her elbow. Carrie catches me looking and readjusts her kimono sleeves.

"From the needles," she explains. "They look a lot worse than they are."

I'm too embarrassed to say anything else.

Another woman stands at the counter, buttering toast. Her hair is growing back in fuzzy patches all over her head. I can't stop staring at her face. There's something weird about it, but I can't put my finger on what. When I finally realize it's because she has no eyebrows or eyelashes, I feel bad for staring and I look away quickly. I read about that happening in one of the pamphlets Mom gave me before I threw it away. If it bothers her, she doesn't act like it.

"I'm sorry we don't have anything exotic, like bacon or eggs," she says wistfully. "I used to love the smell of bacon frying. Now it just makes me nauseous. Ah, well. *C'est la vie!* Toast?"

I take a plate of toast, butter it and sprinkle the whole thing with cinnamon sugar. Joanne and Carrie shove over to make room for Mom and me at the table.

"Thanks, Susan," my mother says to the bacon-lover with no eyebrows.

I eat and the ladies sip their tea in silence for awhile.

"Clarissa drove all the way up from home last night to surprise me," Mom says, winding my ponytail around her finger. She hasn't done that in ages. It's comforting.

"She doesn't look old enough to drive," Joanne says, brushing my cheek with her finger. I flinch only a little. "What's your secret, love?"

"Denise drove," I explain.

"Denise is my oldest and dearest friend," Mom adds. "We left her upstairs sawing logs like an old lumberjack."

The ladies chuckle.

"Is this your first visit to Hopestead?" Susan asks from the counter, where she spoons loose tea leaves into a bag.

I don't say anything but I nod, aware that my mouth is full of toast and not wanting to seem rude to these polite women. I can't remember when I ever had such a polite meal.

"This is my third time at Hopestead," Joanne says. "And you know what they say, third time's a charm."

"So, your cancer came back?" I ask. Somehow I don't feel so bad about asking her questions.

"Unfortunately," she says. "First time in my left breast, second time in my right, now I'm afraid it's found its way into my lung." She leans close to me and lowers her voice. "Persistent little bugger, isn't it?"

Susan frowns. "Don't scare the poor thing, Jo," she scolds. To me she says, "Don't worry. Not everyone relapses."

"But it is a fact that some do," Joanne adds. "No need to lie to the girl. Clarissa here looks like she's made of the strong stuff."

"She is," Mom says.

I feel about ten feet tall. And very grown up.

Joanne gestures at her chest. It's then I notice that her bathrobe hangs flat where the other women's robes curve out from their bodies. "All this is a very small part of my life," she says. "It's never stopped me. Did you know that last year I travelled to Costa Rica? I rode horses in the surf and I even tried zip lining."

"Really?" I ask, unable to picture this woman flying down a mountain on a thick wire.

Joanne nods. "And the year before I ran a half-marathon."

Even if you don't like running, you have to admit that's pretty impressive. Joanne looks like she is at least sixty years old. Maybe older.

"Don't expect me to take up running," Mom says. "Although it might be nice to go on a trip."

My heart leaps. "Really?" I ask.

Mom smiles and nods. "Why not?" she says. "We've never really been anywhere."

"That's the spirit," Joanne says.

The women chat about all sorts of things, comparing T-cell counts, asking after family members, arguing about some TV show they've all been watching. It isn't all cancer this, cancer that. They laugh and joke like they're just a normal group of friends having a normal breakfast. But something has been bothering me. I wait until Susan and Carrie leave, and Mom is clearing the dishes.

"Can I ask you one more thing?" I ask Joanne.

Joanne leans close to me, like she's about to share a secret. "Anything," she says.

"Aren't you angry?" I ask.

Joanne thinks for a moment before answering. "I used to be. I used to be very angry, indeed. And there are still some days where I want to slap someone hard across the face or scream 'why me' at the top of my lungs. But so many good things have come of it all. I know that's very hard to believe, but it's true. If I hadn't been diagnosed with cancer, I may have been content to sit on my fat bottom and never go anywhere or do anything my whole life. Sometimes you need a little hardship in life to get the blood flowing. Just think, if I hadn't been diagnosed, I never would have come to Hopestead and met such good friends," Joanne says. "My mother taught me there is always a silver lining. You just have to look for it. I think it pays to think positively, don't you agree, Clarissa?"

"Yes," I agree.

Joanne winks.

"Smart girl."

Bittersweet

Before she has to check in at the clinic, Mom and I go for a long walk. It's one of those perfect winter days where the sun is bright and the air is crisp but not too cold, and you can almost believe that spring is just around the corner. Hopestead is in a nice neighbourhood with nice looking houses. Families are coming and going, off to get groceries or go to work. People raise their hands and say good morning as we pass by, like we're regular neighbours and not strangers who are staying in the cancer house. It feels good.

"The other women seem nice," I say. "Especially Joanne."

Mom smiles. "I thought you would like her. She's one of my favourites, too. An amazing woman, full of spunk. She reminds me of you."

I don't know how an old British lady with cancer can possibly remind my mother of me, but I like that she's been thinking about me. And I like that she called me spunky and not moody. I want to tell her that I'm sorry I didn't listen when she called every night, and that I'm sorry I seemed so disinterested in her life at Hopestead. Instead I say, "I'm glad that you have friends here."

"Me too. They've been very helpful. But enough about me, I want to hear about you. Tell me what I've missed."

It's easier to talk about things when you're walking. Maybe because you can keep your eyes on where you're going, and you don't have to look someone in the eye and feel them staring at you and judging you — or worse, feeling sorry for you. I tell her about Benji and Terry DiCarlo, Denise almost burning the house down and how Michael Greenblat won't leave me alone and now everyone thinks I have a crush on him. I don't tell her about Mr. Campbell or the letters. She doesn't interrupt and waits until I'm finished before saying, "You've been busy. Anything else on your mind?"

I wonder if Denise told her about my (ugh) *period*, because she seems to know that I'm holding the most important thing back. Or maybe it's just a mom thing. So I take a deep breath and tell her about history class, and Mattie finding me in the bathroom, and faking sick to go home. When I'm finished she turns in the middle of the sidewalk and wraps me in a big hug.

"I'm sorry I wasn't there," she says.

"It's okay," I say, even though it's not.

"No," Mom insists. "It isn't okay. None of this is okay. I should be there for this stuff. I want to be there for this stuff."

For one horrible moment I think she might cry. I don't know what I would do if my mother burst into tears in the middle of the street. "It's not your fault," I say. "It's not like you wanted to get cancer and miss the worst day of my life."

She laughs and throws an arm around my shoulder. We keep walking.

"Oh Clarissa, I've missed you. I miss you every second of every day. Let's get you a treat. Something to celebrate your transition into womanhood."

Ugh. I cover my ears with my hands but even my mittens

are aren't thick enough to block out those words.

"Mom!" I protest. *"Please!"*

Mom laughs.

"Okay, okay. Not celebrate then, how about commemorate?"

"Why would I want to remember it?" I protest.

"Hmm." Mom thinks about it. "What if it was to celebrate that the worst day of your life is over and done with?"

"Can I have a coffee? A tall one with chocolate and whipped cream?"

"I think you mean a mocha," she points out.

"Whatever."

"Yes. As a new woman on the road to adulthood, you may have a mocha."

"I accept."

We shake.

***

Denise and I stay again on Friday night and take Mom out to the mall on Saturday. There is something so normal about listening to Mom and Denise argue about the price of jeans that I forget how much I hate shopping and have a great time. I am totally willing to spend another night, but Denise doesn't want us to tire Mom out, so we head home after dinner.

By the time Denise and I pull into the driveway, it's dark. There are no lights, no signs of life over at Benji's house. The curtains are absolutely still, so I know that he isn't sitting there watching for me. My good mood sags a little bit. I was looking forward to seeing him.

Denise slams the car door and fumbles with the keys.

"Let's go, kiddo," she says. "Mini-break's over. I'm pretty

sure we left dishes in the sink. It's going to take a minor explosion to get the crud off."

"What do you mean 'we?' You're the one who put the dishes in the sink without rinsing them."

"Clarissa," Denise's voice has that warning note in it that Mom gets when she means business. If you ask me, she's taking this temporary guardian thing way too seriously.

I point out that I have homework to catch up on and Denise gives me a murderous glare.

"Fine," she says, "then you can call your little friend, get the assignment and sit in the kitchen and finish it while I do the dishes."

But we never get that far. When we get inside the red light on the answering machine is flashing, and when I press *play* Mattie Cohen's voice bounces around the kitchen.

"Clarissa, it's Mattie. I don't know where you are but I thought I should call you and tell you that Benji was beat up really badly today and taken away in an ambulance. Call me as soon as you get this."

Beat up

There is no answer at Benji's house. I hang up and call again, just in case the Dentonator was sleeping the first time and didn't hear the phone. Still no answer. I slam the receiver in its cradle.

"No answer?" Denise asks.

I glare at her.

"Obviously!"

"He's probably at the hospital."

"Thanks a lot, now I feel much better."

"Did you try your friend Mattie?"

"She is not my friend and no, I did not, because half of what she says is made up anyway."

I can't believe that Benji is really in the hospital. It doesn't seem right. No matter how I try, I just can't picture an ambulance coming and taking him away. I wonder who rode with him to the hospital. I feel sick thinking about it.

"You have to call the hospital!" I shout at Denise.

"They don't just give out patient information, you know," Denise starts. But when she sees how serious I am, she throws her hands up and says, "Okay, okay. Just don't bite my head off when they tell me to get lost."

The phone rings and rings. Why isn't anyone picking up? I can barely stand it.

"What's taking so long?"

Denise shushes me. Finally someone picks up and Denise puts on her best professional woman voice.

"Yes, hello. I'm calling about a patient. Last name Denton, first name Benjamin, but everyone calls him Benji. He would have come in yesterday. Yes, yes, thank you."

Denise hangs up.

"Well?"

"He's not there."

"Not there?"

"He must be at home, probably asleep, poor lamb."

I rush over to the window and search Benji's house for any signs of life. Nothing.

"I'm going over there," I say.

Denise puts out an arm and stops me.

"Honey, maybe it's better to wait till morning."

"I can't wait that long! I need to find out how he is! He may be dying!"

Denise bites her lip and for a second I think she's going to stop me, but instead she sighs and steps aside.

"Okay, but if no one answers, don't go breaking the door down. You come straight home and—"

But I don't hear the rest of what she says. I'm already out the door.

***

At first there's no answer. I ring the bell and bang on the door as loud as I can, and when that's not enough, I kick the door with the toe of my boot. Finally a light comes on and the Dentonator opens the door.

"Clarissa," he says. "Christ, I thought the apocalypse was here."

"I need to see Benji."

David Denton shakes his head and steps out onto the porch, closing the door behind him.

"He's asleep," he says.

"But it's not even nine," I protest.

"He's had a rough couple of days."

My breath catches in my throat.

"Is he okay?"

"Well, he looks like a kid who's been in a fight, but he'll be okay. No permanent damage."

The words permanent damage make me feel queasy.

"What about temporary damage?" I ask.

"He'll live. I've seen a lot worse in my day."

I had almost forgotten I was talking to Benji's dad, the famous Dentonator, former hockey star, genuine tough guy.

"But you were a hockey player," I protest. "You probably started half those fights. Benji doesn't believe in fighting."

"No, he doesn't, and frankly I didn't think he had it in him."

"What do you mean?"

"I mean he may not have thrown the first punch, but he definitely started the fight. And from what he tells me, the other guy deserved it. Looks like you rubbed off on him."

Now I'm totally confused.

The Dentonator looks at me, I mean really looks at me, before continuing.

"You're a good friend to my boy," he says. "I know you've put yourself on the line for him in the past. You come back Monday; I know he'll be happy to see you."

Then he puts his hand on my shoulder, squeezes it and slips back into the darkness of the house.

Blood

"There you are! Where have you *been?* Didn't you get my message? I have so much to tell you!"

Before I can answer any of her questions, Mattie grabs the sleeve of my coat and pulls me behind the tire swings where we can talk privately before the bell rings. To be honest, I'm actually kind of glad, because ever since I arrived at school people have been staring at me and whispering.

"Well?" Mattie demands.

"I went to visit my mother," I say. "Not that it's any of your business."

Mattie's eyes immediately go all soft.

"Is she okay?" she asks.

"Well, as good as one can be on chemo," I retort.

Mattie nods knowingly.

"Chemotherapy is very difficult on your body," she says, like she knows something about it. I resist the urge to say something snappy back.

"What happened on Friday?" I ask.

"You mean with Benji?"

"Of course, with Benji!"

"So you *did* get my message. I wasn't sure because you never called me back."

I can't believe Mattie is getting all sulky at a time like this. I am *thisclose* to walking away, except she is the only one who I can talk to about Benji. I clench my teeth and force myself to smile at her. As Mom says, you catch more flies with honey than with vinegar.

"Sorry Mattie, I was just overwhelmed with my Mom and Benji and everything."

I sound fake, even to myself, but Mattie buys it anyway, making her sad eyes at me and patting my arm.

"Oh my goodness, of course! This must be so hard for you."

I nod and wait for her to continue.

"Well. So, as you know, Friday was the day Mr. Campbell was going to pick the top three modern hero essays and read sections from them aloud."

Oh no! The essay — I had forgotten all about it. You would think Mr. Campbell would have pulled me aside to remind me, or at the very least sent a stern letter home. Instead, he was just going to let me fail. Jerk.

"The first one he read was Julie Kennedy's. I mean, he didn't say so, they were all anonymous, but it was all about Dr. Wellington and the animal rescue centre. Everyone knows how crazy Julie is about animals and that she volunteers there on the weekends. It was pretty obvious.

"The next one was about some baseball player who gives all his money to charity and adopted like, three kids from China. I think it was Michael Greenblat's essay, but that one I'm not sure about. And then he read Benji's."

I swear my heart stopped beating for a second. The thought of Mr. Campbell reading aloud to the whole class what Benji had written about my mother made me want to turn around, run home and never come back to school. Those were personal, private things. How dare he share them with the entire class! What kind of a teacher was he? I was aware of Mattie staring at me, but I didn't trust my voice to work.

"Did you hear me Clarissa? The next one he read was Benji's. Oh, Clarissa, it was so beautiful. Almost all the girls in the class cried."

"I can't believe him!"

Mattie is confused.

"Who?" she asks.

"Both of them!" I yell. "Putting my mom's life on display! We aren't entertainment! This isn't a reality TV show!"

"What are you talking about? It wasn't about your mom, Clarissa. It was about you."

"What?"

Mattie's hands fly up to her mouth.

"You mean you didn't know?" she cries. "That makes it even more tragic!"

For a second I think she's going to burst into tears. I grab her arms to shake some sense into her.

"Mattie! Focus! What did he say?"

"He said that you were the bravest person he knew, always sticking up for people, putting on a brave face even though your mother had cancer and might die—"

"She's not going to die—"

"I'm just telling you what he said! And then he talked about Terry DiCarlo and all the things he did, what a bully he was and how, from now on, he was going to stand up for himself because of you! Oh Clarissa, it was *sooo* inspiring."

I can barely process this new and surprising information. I had read Benji's essay. It was about Mom, not me.

"And then what happened?" I ask.

"Well, obviously we all knew it was Benji's essay. No one else likes you that much, no offence, plus his face was totally red. And then, right before lunch, Mr. Campbell asked Benji to stay behind for a minute."

Mattie pauses for effect and looks at me like maybe it might dawn on me.

"So?"

Mattie rolls her eyes.

"So, the next thing you know, Terry DiCarlo is called to the principal's office and suspended. Because of Benji's essay! Well, he was mad as anything, as you can imagine, and so after school him and a couple of his friends were waiting for Benji."

Mattie takes a deep breath and looks like she might cry again. The thought of Benji walking home alone, unprotected makes me want to cry, too.

"Poor Benji. He didn't stand a chance. I wasn't there, but I heard from someone who saw the whole thing that he actually tried to fight them off."

I feel a surge of pride for Benji.

"Luckily someone ran and got the principal, but by the time he got there, Terry and his gang were gone and Benji was lying on the ground."

Mattie leans forward for the next part.

"They had to wash his blood off the sidewalk," she whispers. I shiver.

"When the ambulance came, the police asked if anyone had seen the attacker. Everyone said no."

"What? But I thought you said it was Terry!" I cry.

"Well, that's what people said, but no one's coming forward to say anything. Don't you get it? Benji wrote about Terry in his essay and look what happened to him."

"Well isn't that proof enough?" I ask.

Mattie shrugs.

"They need a witness. Besides, it happened off school property."

"What about Benji? What does he say?"

"Well, that's the strange thing. You'd think that Benji would've told the police and Terry would have been arrested or thrown in juvie or whatever by now. But he hasn't. That means Benji isn't saying anything."

I frown.

"That doesn't make sense," I say.

"Maybe he's afraid," Mattie suggests. "You weren't there. It wasn't your brains getting bashed in."

"You weren't there either," I remind her.

Mattie's lip wobbles.

"I'm just telling you what happened," she says hotly.

My head is spinning with all this information. I don't know what to do with it. When the bell rings, I am thankful. At least now I can sit in math class and zone out so I can think it all over.

***

I am an overnight sensation. People I don't even know smile at me in the hall. One girl comes up to me and says, "Hang in there, Clarissa." I've never talked to her before in my life! With Terry gone, the school seems friendlier and happier. More people are laughing in the hallways. It's like Munchkinland when Dorothy drops the house on the Wicked Witch of the East; suddenly everyone's singing and in Technicolor. I can't believe how many people hate Terry. It makes me mad that none of them did anything about it. I am starting to feel a little guilty about all the kudos and congratulations, though. After all, I didn't do anything. It was Benji who wrote the essay; he's the one who put it all out there. Correction, stupid Mr. Campbell put it out there for him. Cripes, how dumb can you be? Of course Terry DiCarlo is going to come for Benji after that!

For Benji's sake, I decide to give Mr. Campbell the silent treatment and I am sure to glare at him extra hard when his back is turned. But he is having none of it. In fact, he smiles extra big when he sees me.

"Clarissa! Good to have you back. The classroom is so peaceful and dull without you."

I nod but refuse to speak.

"Unfortunately, you missed a busy day, but I trust Miss Mattie will answer any of your questions about the homework."

Mattie smiles brightly.

"Yes, Mr. Campbell," she says.

Ugh.

"And if you don't mind, I'd love for you to stay after class today. I want to return your assignment and talk to you about a few things. I'd see you at lunch, but I have a meeting."

I shrug and slide into my seat.

"I'm sorry Clarissa, I didn't hear you," Mr. Campbell says. He says it nice enough, but there's an edge underneath that means business.

"Sure thing, Mr. C. After school," I say.

"Grrrrreat!"

***

I miss Benji the most at lunchtime. Not because I'm alone, in fact I've never sat with so many people at lunch before in my entire life. Mattie leads the pack of girls who plunk right down beside me at the table. They keep saying "how brave"

I am, and that they're, "praying for Benji and your mom." When it becomes clear that I'm not about to share any juicy secrets, they sort of forget I'm there and talk among themselves about boys and some TV show I've never heard of because we only watch old reruns at my house.

Across the cafeteria, Michael Greenblat keeps looking over at me. I know he won't dare come talk to me in front of all these girls, but I find myself wishing he would. Even geodes are better than all this talk about boys.

"Oh my God, Clarissa, Michael Greenblat is totally checking you out!" Amanda says. "What's going on?"

I shrug.

"It's nothing," I say. "We're sort of friends."

The girls all look at each other and something passes between them that I must have missed, because they all start giggling.

"Sure," says Min, rolling her eyes, "friends." And then she dissolves into more giggles.

Benji isn't a giggler.

Busted

The last bell goes and people grab their books and bolt for the door. It's what I would be doing if I hadn't been asked to stay behind to have a chat with Mr. Campbell.

"I'll wait for you," Mattie offers.

I wave her off.

"Don't bother."

"Call me!" Mattie says.

I shrug, which is not exactly a no, but it's not a yes, either. Mr. Campbell sits at his desk and rifles through a pile of papers. He doesn't even look up at me. Two can play this game. I take out the homework from Friday and pretend to get started on that. Every once in awhile I steal a glance through my eyelashes, but Mr. Campbell hasn't moved. He clears his throat, but when I look up he still has his nose buried in those papers.

After what seems like a year, he stops what he's doing and smiles at me like he hadn't noticed I was right there in front of him for ten whole minutes.

"Clarissa," he says, folding his hands in front of him. "Clarissa Louise Delaney."

I don't like it when people use my full name, it makes me nervous. Not that I would ever let him know that. I smile brightly and say in my most chipper voice, "Yes, Mr. Campbell?"

Mr. Campbell reaches into his desk and pulls out a fat folder. He walks over, tosses it on my desk and says, "I need your help with something. I received this from Principal Donner the other day. Take a look at these and tell me what you would do if you were in my position."

"Okay."

I open the folder and find a pile of letters staring up at me. I recognize them right away. *Dear Principal Donner, I am writing to issue a formal complaint about a Mr. Campbell . . . my child comes home crying everyday because of something that Mr. Campbell has said . . . Mr. Campbell is a lazy and incompetent teacher . . . I have three children and never has any of them complained about a teacher more than my son has complained about Mr. Campbell.* Reading them over, I can't believe I was so mean. The letters are so angry, so full of hate. I am so ashamed that I can't look up at him.

"Well? What would you do?" he asks quietly.

I don't trust myself to say anything.

"You know, it's hard being the new guy," Mr. Campbell says. "Especially when the shoes you're trying to fill are so big. I gather Miss Ross was pretty out of this world."

He waits for me to say something, but all I can manage is a shrug. When he speaks again his voice is quiet.

"Tell me about her."

And so I tell him about the bird's nest, and how she brought me to this very room and told me I was an eagle and I believed her. I tell him how I had waited and waited for this year, and now that it is here and I am living it, nothing has gone the way I planned. As the truth comes out I realize that if Miss Ross knew about the letters she would be ashamed of me. I am ashamed of me. I feel less like an eagle and more like a worm.

"An eagle," Mr. Campbell says.

I nod, feeling exposed and embarrassed, but Mr. Campbell doesn't laugh. He doesn't say anything; he just looks at me thoughtfully.

"You're a good mimic, Clarissa, and a great writer. In fact, I wish you would put as much effort into your assignments as you did into these letters. But you're not that good. Principal Donner and I thought a lot about what we should do about these, about what sort of punishment would be appropriate. I asked her to leave it up to me."

Here it comes. I take a shaky breath and wait for the axe to fall. I'll be suspended, held back a year, or worse, he'll show my mother and she'll take back all those things she said about being proud of me.

"The thing is," Mr. Campbell continues, "I think you've been punished enough."

What? There has to be a catch. When I look up, Mr. Campbell puts his big chin in his hands and looks right at me.

"You've had a rough year, Clarissa." When I don't say anything, he says, "Well? Haven't you?"

Somehow I find my voice. "Yes, sir."

Mr. Campbell laughs. "Sir! Now I know you're feeling out of sorts. See, the thing is, I know these aren't really about me," Mr. Campbell taps the letters littered all over my desk. "They're about your mom, Benji, Miss Ross and everything else, but they aren't about me. When I read your essay, I finally got a glimpse of what's going on up there."

Mr. Campbell points at my head. I'm confused. What essay? What is he talking about?

"I want you to know that I am not the enemy here. If you need to talk about something, if you want to yell and scream, you can come to me. And in the meantime, we're going to make a deal. I will forget I ever saw those letters, and in return you will help out with the Lunchtime Lineup from now until the end of school. Put those writing skills to good use and find me some interesting stories about the students and the staff right here at Ferndale. You certainly have a flair for dramatics, there's no doubt about that, but this is your chance to make a difference."

He can't be serious. It's too good to be true. As lame as the student radio station is, it's better than detention or suspension.

"Well? Do we have a deal?"

Mr. Campbell offers me his hand. I shake it, and he smiles.

"A wise choice, Clarissa. Now, let's get rid of the evidence, shall we?"

And with that, he sweeps the letters off my desk and dumps them into the recycling bin.

"Before you go, here's your essay back. And for what it's worth, I think you should show your mother. I think she'd be very touched."

I take my essay from him, except it's not my essay at all. It has a drawing of my mom on it, with the title *Annette Delaney: Local Wonder Woman* written just like the comic book across the top. It's Benji's original essay, except on the bottom, Benji has erased his name and replaced it with mine.

***

Benji is sitting in bed with a whole stack of pillows propping him up, watching the TV his dad brought in and set up on his dresser. His left eye is still puffy looking, but the bruise has started to turn yellow and green at the edges. There is a cut in his lip and his right arm is held across his body in a sling.

Benji lists off his injuries. Each one makes me angrier and angrier.

"Cracked rib, black eye, minor concussion. You know, regular hockey type injuries."

Benji smiles at his own joke, then winces, touching his lip gently.

"Here, I brought this for you," I say, handing him a makeup bag full of concealer, foundation and correction sticks. "So you can do your face up for school tomorrow." "Thanks, but I'm not sure if I'm ready to go back yet," Benji says. "Besides, I was thinking of going *au naturel*. Everybody knows anyway."

"Hey Benji, how come the principal is still looking for the people who beat you up?"

Benji looks down but doesn't say anything.

"Didn't you tell anybody?"

"They'd think I was a tattletale."

"I heard all about your essay, Benji, the whole school did! Terry already thinks you're a tattletale. The difference is now you can really get him."

Benji chews thoughtfully on his Oreo and refuses to look at me.

"What is it, are you afraid?"

"Look at my face, Clarissa. Of course, I'm afraid."

"But everyone knows now, the teachers, everyone. You're safer now than ever."

"I'm not afraid for me, I'm afraid for you. Terry told me that if I said anything to anyone they'd come after you."

A little warning bell goes off in my head but I ignore it. Surely he wasn't serious. Terry DiCarlo is an idiot, but he can't be that stupid.

"And you believed him? I'm a girl; he'd never do anything to me. And no offence, Benji, but I'm a better runner than you are. I can outrun Terry and his friends."

Benji shakes his head.

"You weren't there, Clarissa. You don't know how crazy Terry can get."

I don't really want to know how crazy that is, and from the way Benji fidgets with the edge of his blanket, I can tell he doesn't really want to get into it, either.

"There's something else I wanted to talk to you about," I say, changing the subject. "Mr. Campbell gave me my essay back, or I should say, he gave me your essay back."

Benji squirms.

"Why did you do that?" I demand.

"You didn't tell him, did you?" he asks.

"No! But I should have. He knows about the letters, Benji. He kept me after school and asked me what I thought he should do about them."

"What did you say?"

I throw my hands up.

"Nothing! What was I supposed to say?"

"Did you cry?"

"No, I did not cry . . . although I thought I might," I admit.

"I would have cried for sure."

"Well, that's not saying much, you cry at everything. The point is, he knew it was me, and instead of punishing me, all I have to do is collect material for the stupid Lunchtime Lineup. Can you believe it?"

"Yes," Benji says. "I like Mr. Campbell. He came with me to the hospital, you know."

This bit of information is new and surprising.

"Really?" I ask.

Benji nods.

"Yup. And he stayed with me until Dad showed up. I think he might be the nicest person I know. Besides your mom. Too bad he's already married; they would make the world's nicest couple."

I roll my eyes.

"Great. And now he thinks I wrote an essay that you actually wrote, which makes me a liar, and he wants me to show it to my mom."

I sit up as a horrible thought occurs to me.

"What if he shows it to her on parent-teacher night?"

"He gave it back to you, right?" Benji points out.

I sigh and fall back on the pillows.

"Right. Phew. That was close."

"So, you're not going to tell him?"

"I don't know yet. I got an A."

"You mean *I* got an A."

"Right, whatever. Besides, I think if he had read my Oprah essay he probably would have punished me way harder."

"Well, I won't tell if you won't," Benji says.

"You still haven't told me why you did it."

Benji shrugs.

"You had a lot going on. I knew you'd forgotten all about it."

"So?"

"So, I didn't want you to get in trouble. Besides, it was already finished."

Sometimes you love a person so much that you can never find the words to tell them without sounding goofy or fake. If I hadn't bawled my eyes out a few days ago, or maybe if I were Mattie Cohen, I'd be crying right now and hugging Benji's boney little body so hard he'd be one big bruise. But I am Clarissa Louise Delaney, so instead I look him right in the eyes and tell him, "You can borrow my homework whenever you need to for the rest of our lives until we're done school." I hope he gets that I mean so much more than that.

Broadcasting

When Mr. Campbell assigned me to the Lunchtime Lineup, I thought, well, it'll be boring, not to mention a total waste of my lunch hour, but how bad can it be? Anything is better than having to tell my mom what I did, or having to tell her what I did and being suspended, too, right? Wrong. Mr. Campbell forgot to tell me that for the rest of the year I am basically going to be Jessica Riley's personal slave.

Jessica Riley is the queen of grade eight, and, therefore, the entire school. At least she thinks she is. But having blond hair with a natural wave and being president of student council does not make you queen of everything. Not that I would ever tell Jessica that. It's easier just to nod and do what she tells me. Later, at home, I do impressions of her for Benji. He thinks they're hilarious. I can only do one or two, though, because he laughs so hard his bruised rib hurts. I think doing impressions is excellent training for when I am an actress.

At first Jessica was excited to have "an assistant," and she flitted around the radio station pointing everything out to me. But since I'm not allowed to touch any of the sound or recording equipment, I didn't pay very much attention.

"This is a *very important job*," Jessica had said, speaking slowly so that I understood just how important the job is.

"We are the voice of Ferndale. The student body relies on us to bring them interesting stories that they can relate to. Like the piece I did on the orphans in cages in Romania."

Even though I was dying to, I didn't ask how we, the students of Ferndale, were supposed to relate to babies in Romania. I bet most people couldn't even point to Romania on a map. I know I can't. I also bit my tongue and refrained from reminding her that particular story made at least three people cry, and that Mr. Campbell had asked the Lunchtime Lineup crew to focus on local issues from then on. I didn't say any of this. All I said was, "Right."

"So, do you have any leads?" Jessica asked me. I shrugged. Jessica cocked her head to one side in a way she probably thinks is cute. When she spoke again, her voice was sticky-sweet. "I was thinking maybe I could do a story about your mom. Maybe I can interview you and your mom together, you know, about your experience."

"No."

Jessica smiled and patted me on the shoulder. She has a lot of very white teeth. Like a shark. "Of course," she said. "This must be a very hard time for you."

I'd shaken her hand off my shoulder and glared at her. Her smile disappeared and she turned and flipped through her binder, which is covered in pictures of boys cut from magazines. Barf. Without looking up, she said, "Well, if you don't have anything to offer, you can make yourself useful and get sound bites about March Break. You know, what people are doing, are they going on a trip, blah, blah, blah. And don't get too many grade sevens. They can barely string a sentence together."

I pretended not to hear that the last bit and slipped the handheld recorder into my backpack. "Anything else?" I asked sweetly.

"Yes," Jessica said. "Get me a Diet Coke."

And so my punishment began.

***

Back when Lunchtime Lineup was new, people used to run up to Jessica or whoever had the recorder to give their opinions. Now people are pretty bored of it, and I practically have to beg them to talk into the microphone. At first it was hard walking up to a group of people and interrupting them for an interview, but it's gotten easier. Sometimes Mattie tags along. She loves talking to people, even strangers.

"Hi, there! We're with Lunchtime Lineup. Can we get a moment of your time?"

I guess something about her enthusiasm is contagious — I always have more luck when she's around. When she's not with me, I pretend to be her: perky and smiley and totally committed to the show. It usually works, even though I feel like a phoney the whole time. The other kids don't seem to notice.

Most of the stories aren't very exciting: 6A has raised $1000 for the Alzheimer Society, the floor hockey team is having a bake sale, auditions for the school musical are coming soon. But sometimes I'll be talking to someone, and they'll have a really cool story. Like a few days ago, I was talking to a kid in grade six whose family just adopted a baby girl from China. Today, I met this other kid whose dad had been an Olympic curler. I mean, it's not like he was a famous hockey player, or one of those skiers who does crazy tricks in the air, but still, he went to the Olympics. I thought that interview was pretty good. But no matter how lame or how cool the story is, Jessica barely acknowledges me.

"Just leave it on the desk and I'll get Mike to edit it," she says. Then she adds, "I hope we can use it."

Bonding

In class, I pass Mattie a note during a movie on the life cycle of the salmon. In order to get it to Mattie, I first have to pass it to Min who looks at Mattie's name in my handwriting and then whips around in her seat to stare at me. Her eyebrows go up.

"Is your name Mattie?" I hiss.

She frowns and rolls her eyes.

"No, obviously."

"Well then, keep passing!"

Min taps Mattie on the shoulder and slips her the note. Mattie takes it, grins and immediately pretends to be studying her science book, letting her hair fall over the page. Nosy-Parker Min leans as far forward in her chair as possible, trying to get a glimpse of the letter, but Mattie is a pro. As much as Mattie loves passing notes, she hates to get caught, so she has perfected the sneaky art of reading a note in class.

After a second she scribbles a reply and leans back and pretends to ask Min for a pencil, slipping her the note. Min passes it back under my desk and I grab it, opening it to read Mattie's reply, written in pink pen, underneath my original message:

Dear Mattie, Would you like to come over after school? From Clarissa.

I would love to!!! I just have to ask my mom!!! This will be soooo fun!!

Cripes. Even her handwriting is perky.

When I look up, Mattie is smiling and waving at me. But then Mr. Campbell clears his throat and she whips around, immediately engrossed in the salmon jumping up the river. I bet if you gave her the choice between being a teacher's pet and being the coolest girl in school, she would pick teacher's pet. Once a goody two-shoes, always a goody two-shoes. I hope I haven't made a mistake. I'm sort of relying on Mattie to help me with a plan I've been cooking up to get Terry DiCarlo once and for good. I guess I'll find out after school.

***

"So, have you seen Benji? Is he okay? When is he coming back to school?"

"Yes, sort of and I don't know."

"Was anything broken?"

"No, but his shoulder was dislocated and he cracked a rib."

"I've never broken a bone in my life. My mom says the pain is unbearable. I have a very low threshold for pain. I don't think I could stand it. That's why I always drink lots of milk and I stay away from contact sports."

"What about dance?"

Mattie frowns

"What *about* dance?" she asks.

"Couldn't you break a bone in dance class?"

"No, I'm more likely to strain something. Besides dance isn't a sport, it's more of an art form."

Mattie hasn't stopped talking since we left the school. She jabbers on about anything and everything: the weather, her mom, her new coat, broken bones. It's exhausting. I just answer her questions, mostly. Benji and I can hang out together for hours without saying more than a few words. Maybe that's what happens when you know someone for a long time: you don't need to talk so much because you know what they're thinking. With Mattie, everything is new. And apparently everything is up for conversation.

"Ooh, is this where you live? It's so cute!"

"You think so?"

I look at my house and try to see it like Mattie does. It's not very big, just one storey, plus the basement. It's made of pinkish bricks, with a white door, white shutters and white blinds in the windows. In the spring Mom plants red geraniums in the flower beds, but in the winter the garden is bare and she wraps the bushes in burlap bags to keep them safe from the wind and snow. On the front door a sign is mounted just below the knocker that says *Guests of the Hair Emporium: Please Enter Through Side Door to the Left of the House.* I remember when Mom made the sign, sitting at the kitchen table and carefully painting the letters in a pretty shade of purple that I had helped her pick.

I take Mattie in through the side door and, because she asks, I give her the grand tour.

"There isn't much to see," I say, but Mattie doesn't seem to think so. She points at all the pictures on the mantle, wanting to know the names of the people in them, looks at my mom's books and magazines, asks to see our movie collection. She even comments on the fabric of the throw pillows in the basement.

"My mom made them out of her old concert T-shirts," I explain.

"Really? Cool!" Mattie says.

"Yeah, it is," I agree, and I realize that I actually mean it.

"Can I see your room?" she asks, so I take her in and stand back while she examines everything, from the bed ("You have a captain's bed? I always wanted a bed with drawers underneath!"), my desk ("Everything's so neat and organized! My mom would love you!") and the clothes in my closet ("No offence, Clarissa but you really need to go shopping. You would think the daughter of a hair stylist would be more, well, stylish.").

Mattie hops up onto my bed and lies flat on her back. I sit on the edge of the bed. It's strange to be in here with someone that's not Benji.

"Hey! Do those glow in the dark?" She points at the stars.

"They used to, but not anymore."

"Neither do mine," Mattie says. "Your house is really cool," she adds.

"Thanks."

"And thanks for inviting me over. I didn't think you liked me all that much."

I blush.

"It's not that, it's just—" but she stops me before I finish.

"I know. My mom says I can be a bit much sometimes and I need to relax around people my own age."

Well, what do you say to that? I can't believe Mattie's mom talks to her like that, like she's her therapist.

"Oh. Well. Are you relaxed now?"

Mattie smiles and bounces a little on the bed.

"Yeah, I am!"

"Good. Because I need your help."

And so I let her in on The Plan.

***

When I finish explaining The Plan, I expect Mattie to jump up and run all the way home. Instead she claps her hands and bounces on the bed again.

"It's perfect!" she cries. "Justice is served!"

"Really? You'll help?" I can't hide my surprise. I mean, I was hoping she'd help out, but it requires her to break about five zillion of her goody two-shoes rules. Mattie stops bouncing and looks offended.

"Of course. Something needs to be done to stop Terror DiCarlo."

"Hey! Terror DiCarlo! That's pretty good!" I say.

Mattie grins.

"I've never called him that out loud before," she admits.

"I like it. Let's call him that from now on."

"Like a codename?"

"Well, it's not that much of a codename. I mean it's pretty obvious."

Mattie's face falls.

"Oh."

"But sure, whatever, when it's just the two of us."

This perks her up a bit.

"Okay! The Matador and Clarissa take on the Terror!"

"The Matador?"

Mattie shrugs, looking a little sheepish.

"That's what I would call myself. Like, if I was a superhero."

"What would my name be?"

Mattie sits back, cocks her head to one side and looks me over, her eyes narrowed.

"Picking a superhero name is very important," she says. "It has to mean something to you, as well as instill fear or awe in whoever utters it."

Wow. She takes this really seriously.

179

"How do you come up with this stuff?" I ask.

Even though there's no one else around, Mattie leans forward and whispers, "Do you really want to know?"

I nod.

"I love comic books," she confesses, and because I can't in a million years picture prissy Mattie Cohen reading a comic book, I throw my head back and laugh. At first Mattie looks offended, but then she loosens up and starts to giggle.

"But don't tell anyone!" she protests.

"I won't, I swear," I say. "Well, maybe just Benji. But he loves comic books. You should see his collection. He even draws his own characters."

"Maybe we could write a comic together," Mattie says.

"Maybe."

"Now, think!" Mattie scolds. "We have to come up with your name. Do you have a favourite superhero?"

I shake my head.

"Not really."

"Favourite animal?"

"Sort of." I hesitate. "I mean, I've always sort of liked eagles."

Mattie beams. "Oooh, eagles are perfect! Powerful and majestic. Now we need to make it snazzier. The Eagle doesn't have enough of a ring to it."

My gaze lands on *The Wonderful Wizard of Oz*, waiting for me on the nightstand.

"What about — the Emerald Eagle?" I suggest.

"Perfect!" Mattie cries. "I can see your costume and everything."

I'm almost afraid to ask.

"Really? What would it look like?"

"Well, green, obviously, with a long feathered cape and talons that retract—"

"Nope, sorry. I'm allergic to feathers."

Mattie's cheek twitches.

"An eagle that's allergic to feathers?"

We stare at each other before bursting into laughter. We roll on the bed, laughing until we can barely breathe. Mattie sits up, wipes the laughter tears from her eyes and says, "Hey Clarissa, can we go see your mom's salon?"

"Sure!"

***

I haven't been in the salon since Mom left. I forgot how cute and sunny it can look. Mattie is practically in heaven, smelling the hair products, testing out the chairs, lining up all the scissors and combs.

"It's so cool you get to live here," she says. "Are you going to be a hairdresser, too?"

"No," I say. "I'm going to be an actress."

It feels weird saying it out loud. I've never told anyone that I want to be an actress, except Benji. I don't know why I told Mattie, the world's largest big mouth, but it just sort of came out. Mattie considers this, looking me up and down.

"My cousin did a commercial once," she says. "All the big movie stars get their start in commercials. But you're prettier than her, so it will probably be easier for you."

"Thanks," I say, but that doesn't seem like enough. Am I supposed to tell her that she's pretty, too? "What about you?"

"I'm going to be a child therapist."

I can feel my eyebrows rise, but I fight to keep them down. As normally as I can, I manage to say, "Oh?"

"Every day my mom sees more and more troubled children come into the hospital. She says the therapists and social workers have their hands full. It's very distressing."

"Wow, that's amazing."

Mattie grins.

"Thanks. I really want to help people."

And as she says it, I realize that it's true. As annoying and bossy as Mattie can be, she's always trying to be helpful. Maybe her problem is that she just isn't helping the right people, or she hasn't figured out the right way to help them. You can't blame a person for that.

"I think you'll be a great child therapist," I say, and I mean it.

Mattie smiles so widely that I can't help but smile back.

"Knock, knock."

Denise is in the doorway, looking quizzically at me. Mattie shoots up out of the chair she's in and marches over to Denise, offering her a hand and a big smile.

"Hi, I'm Mattie Cohen, a friend of Clarissa's from school."

Denise is not as good at keeping her eyebrows under control as I am. They practically disappear into her hairline. She shakes Mattie's hand as she looks over the top of her head at me. I pretend to be looking for dirt under my fingernails.

"From school, of course. I'm Denise Renzetti, a friend of Clarissa's mom's and regional sales manager for Mary Kay cosmetics."

Mattie actually squeals.

"Really? I love Mary Kay!"

Denise is pleased.

"You do?"

Mattie wiggles her fingers at Denise, who inspects her nails.

"Opalescence, shade 46," she announces.

Mattie claps her hands.

"How did you know?"

"Because it's my job! I am a professional."

Cripes.

"Hey, would you girls like a makeover?" Denise asks.

Mattie gasps and her arms start to jiggle at her sides.

"Oh, yes, please! Can we Clarissa?"

"I don't know . . ."

Mattie grabs my arm and pulls on it, jumping up and down.

"Please, please, please? It'll be so fun!"

"Okay, fine. But no liquid eyeliner. I hate liquid eyeliner."

"Not me," says Mattie, eyes shining. "I love it!"

Denise takes off her blazer and pushes the sleeves of her blouse back.

"All right ladies, take a seat. Welcome to La Spa Denise."

She opens her pink briefcase and lets us pick out a shade of nail polish while she runs upstairs to get her arsenal.

I can't tell who is more excited, Denise or Mattie.

"Denise is so cool," Mattie says, tuning the radio to the good station. "Thanks for inviting me!"

I shrug.

"You're welcome."

"This is going to be so fun!"

And, surprisingly, it is.

When Denise is in Mary Kay mode she spends less time making bad jokes and complaining about her love life. Instead, she talks about the importance of shading your cheekbones, blending the right shade of concealer and making your eyes pop.

"It's like painting," Mattie says.

Denise approves.

"It's exactly like painting," she agrees. "You need to prep your canvas and use the right brushes for the desired effect."

Denise bustles between Mattie and me, scrutinizing our

pores and moving our chins this way and that to assess our angles. She turns our chairs around so we can't watch our progress in the mirror.

"You don't want to spoil the reveal," she scolds.

"Just like on TV!" says Mattie.

I start to get impatient. Denise is taking hours with Mattie's eye makeup. How many coats of mascara does one person need?

"And — done!" she says.

"Can we look?" Mattie asks.

Denise steps back and gestures to the mirror.

"Be my guest!"

Mattie looks at me and grins.

"On three," she says. "One, two, three!"

Wow. I can't believe that's me in the mirror. My eyes look huge. Whatever shadow Denise used makes them look greenish instead of muddy brown. I never noticed how green my eyes were before. They look pretty.

Mattie fluffs her hair and turns this way and that, examining every inch of her makeover.

"I love it!" she gushes. "I feel like a movie star! I could totally pass for sixteen!"

Sixteen is a little much, but she does look older, and very sophisticated. We both do.

"You look beautiful, Clarissa! Look out Hollywood!"

"So do you," I say.

"Let's take a picture of you girls and we'll send it to your mom," Denise says. "I know she'd love to see you all dolled up, Clarissa."

Mattie throws her arm around me and flashes her best smile. I stiffen a little bit. It's strange to have her standing so close, like we've been best friends forever. Denise frowns.

"For God's sakes, Clarissa, it's not a mug shot."

"Yeah! It's a glamour shot!" Mattie says. Then she whispers in my ear, so that only I can hear, "Matador and the Emerald Eagle take on the world, one eyelash at a time!"

I can't help but smile. Mattie can be pretty goofy sometimes.

"Got it!" Denise says. "Now I just have to figure out how to upload the darn thing and I'll send it tonight."

"Thank you so much, Denise, this was so much fun! I wish I didn't have to take it all off tonight. I'd love to show up at school like this. Can you imagine? Amanda would just die!"

***

"Are you wearing makeup?"

"Yeah, Mattie came over and Denise gave us makeovers."

Benji's eyes practically bug right out of his head.

"Mattie came over?"

"So?"

"And you let Denise touch your face?"

"It's no big deal," I say.

"I feel like the whole world is changing," Benji says. "By the time I get back to school you'll be married to Michael Greenblat."

Normally I would slap him but I restrain myself on account of his injuries. Instead, I ignore the comment, like a mature, responsible person. Maybe it's the makeup seeping through my skin and into my brain, making me more sophisticated.

"When are you coming back?" I ask.

Benji looks uncomfortable.

"I don't know yet," he says.

185

"Well, you can't stay home forever."

"I know that. I think I'm getting the flu."

Benji squirms against the pillows like he's trying to disappear inside them. He gets a faraway look on his face and I know he's thinking about the attack. He still doesn't talk about it. Mrs. Stremecki, the guidance counsellor, told me that when you talk about something that's bothering you, you allow others to share the burden of your pain, and that although it might be hard, it's a relief, too. That was when she was trying to get me to talk about my mother's cancer. Back then I thought it was a load of crap, but now I wonder if maybe there is a slight chance that she wasn't totally and completely wrong.

I wish Benji would tell me what happened, so I could help him with his burden. But for now he just stays in bed with that scared look in his eyes. That look makes my blood boil. It makes me want to kill Terry DiCarlo. But now that Mattie is in on The Plan, things are finally starting to look up.

Baking

On Saturday Mattie comes over for lunch. She shows up in a blouse, vest and kilt with knee socks. I don't think she ever wears pants.

"Let's make cookies and bring them over to Benji!" she says.

"We don't bake things here," I say. "We probably don't have all the stuff you need."

"We can get one of those mixes," Mattie suggests. "Then you just add water, eggs and oil. Everyone has that stuff around. Then you just mix it up and plop it onto a cookie sheet. I've done it a million times."

"I'm pretty sure we don't have a cookie sheet."

Mattie is disgusted.

"How can you not have a cookie sheet? Everyone has a cookie sheet. If only I'd known, I could have brought one of mine."

She has more than one? I rummage around in the drawers under the countertop, the ones we never use. There's an old lime green mixer, Tupperware containers without lids and a dustpan. I'm pretty sure that Mom keeps aluminum pie plates back here somewhere. Aha.

"What about these?" I ask.

Mattie is incredulous.

"You don't have a cookie sheet, but you have a whole bag of pie tins?"

"They're good for mixing hair dyes," I tell her.

Mattie inspects the tins and decides that they will do.

"Now all we need is the mix," she says.

"And eggs," I add.

"Lucky for us they have eggs and cookie mix at the 7-Eleven," she says. "Let's go!"

***

It turns out baking is pretty easy, especially when you have someone telling you what to do. We make a whole batch of delicious, chewy chocolate chip oatmeal cookies with extra chocolate chips. We've added some from a bag because Mattie says that cookie mixes are pretty skimpy on the chocolate. Some of our cookies have so many chips in them that the chocolate has melded together into one big gooey chocolate centre. Heaven. We're letting them cool when the doorbell rings.

I open the door to find Michael Greenblat staring back at me.

"Oh, hi, Clarissa."

"Michael?"

"Sorry I'm late."

I blink.

"Late? For what?"

"Mattie said to come around two."

"Mattie said?"

The next thing I know, Mattie is at my elbow pulling Michael into the house.

"Hi, Michael! I'm so glad you came! Come in."

"But—"

"Want a cookie? Clarissa and I made them."

Mattie holds out the plate of cookies and smiles as Michael grabs two of them and stuffs them in his mouth at once.

"Thanks," he mumbles through a mouthful of cookie. At least I think that's what he said.

"Those were supposed to be for Benji," I say, but Mattie pulls me aside and shushes me as Michael peels off his coat and boots and chucks them by the door.

"*Shhh!* The way to a man's heart is through his stomach."

"What is that supposed to mean? Do you think I like Michael? Because I don't. He's the one who—"

Mattie crosses her arms and rolls her eyes.

"Spare me," she says. "Besides, we need his help."

"With what?"

But then Michael is back, hands in his pockets, hanging around the entrance to the kitchen, like he isn't sure whether or not he should come in. Mattie is all smiles as she bustles over to the kitchen cupboard like she lives here or something.

"Would you like a glass of milk?" she asks.

"Yes, please," he says.

"Maybe we should all sit in the living room," Mattie suggests. "Clarissa, you go with Michael. I'll just get the milk."

I think I'm in shock. Who does she think she is telling me what to do in my own home?

"But—"

"I'll be right behind you."

"Fine." I stomp into the living room, not even bothering to see if Michael is behind me. I feel like a stranger in my own home.

"Sit wherever you like," I say, slumping onto a corner of the couch. I'm too mad to say anything else.

Michael sits on the other end with his hands in his lap. His hair is combed straight back and it looks like there might be gel in it. Michael never uses gel. Plus, he's wearing a plain sweater, a nice one. There isn't a Blue Jays logo in sight. He clears his throat a couple of times before asking, "How's your mom?"

"Okay."

"She comes home soon, right?"

How does he know this?

"A week."

"That's nice. Do you talk to her a lot?"

I shrug.

"I can call her whenever I like."

Michael nods.

"That's good."

What is taking Mattie so long? It's getting harder to think of things to talk about. I'm not sure how much more of this I can stand. Finally she appears, hands Michael a glass of milk and pulls up a dining room chair. She looks very pleased with herself.

"So," she says. "We're gathered here today to talk about the Terry situation."

My jaw drops open.

"You told him?" I say.

Mattie flips her hair over her shoulder.

"We can't do this on our own," she reasons. "Besides, Michael wants to help. Don't you Michael?"

Michael takes a breather from downing the entire glass of milk.

"Terry's a jerk," he says, wiping the milk moustache from his lip with the back of his hand. "I've never liked the guy."

"I can't believe you told him," I say.

Michael looks hurt.

"No offence," I add quickly. "It's just, it was my plan, and it was private, and now Mattie's gone and told everyone."

"Not everyone, just Michael!" Mattie insists.

"I never should have told you," I say.

"Clarissa, you can't do everything on your own."

"I don't!"

"No, you're right. You do everything with *Benji*. You and Benji are like this little club for two," she continues. "You barely talk to anyone else. It's like no one else is good enough for you."

"That's not true," I say, but I can tell by the look on Michael's face that he agrees with Mattie. He turns red and stuffs another one of Benji's cookies in his mouth. All of a sudden it dawns on me. They think we're snobs, that I'm a snob. The thought is so ridiculous it makes me want to laugh.

"Benji's my best friend," I explain.

"So? You can still have other friends," Mattie says.

I don't understand why she cares so much. What have I ever done to her except avoid her and make fun of her behind her back? Why would she want to be friends with me if I'm such a snob? Mattie sighs.

"Look. Your plan is a good one, but we're going to need backup."

"Says you," I grumble.

"Fine. We'll take a vote. All those who think Clarissa Delaney is being a big baby and needs all the help she can get, say aye. Aye!"

Mattie shoots her hand in the air. Michael looks guilty, but his hand goes up and he mumbles something like aye as well.

"That's not fair," I start, but Mattie cuts me off.

"Sorry Clarissa, we live in Canada, and in Canada democracy rules. The people have spoken."

I'm pretty sure she got that one from a video we were forced to watch in history.

"Now, I brought my journal so we can take notes. I'll type them up and email them to everyone after."

***

So my brilliant idea now includes me, Mattie and Michael. Tomorrow is the big day and I am up past midnight, going over The Plan in my head. There are so many things that could go wrong. Before, when it was just me, I was the only person who could screw up. Now there are three people involved, which means there are three times the chances that things could go wrong. Or something like that. All I know is that there are parts of the plan that are out of my hands, and that makes me nervous.

Denise and I decided not to tell Mom about Benji's attack. We both agreed that it would upset her and there was nothing she could do from Hopestead, so it was better to just not mention it until she came home. Part of me is dying to tell her all about The Plan, so I can hear her tell me it's a great idea and everything will turn out fine. But a bigger part of me wants her to concentrate on getting better. She has enough to worry about without imagining Benji all beat up and bruised and me taking on Terror DiCarlo.

The what-ifs keep getting bigger and bigger in my head, until I almost get up, call Mattie and tell her the whole thing is off. I need something to calm me down, something to make me feel powerful again. The Emerald Eagle needs a good luck talisman. I sneak into Mom's room and open the closet door where she keeps her belts hanging on a rack. In the dark they look like dead snakes, nailed there to keep out intruders. Even though I haven't worn it in over a year, I still get the same feeling when I see it: Dorothy's magic belt, hanging there like something ordinary. Benji and I used to pretend that no harm could come to the person wearing the belt. It was good luck charm, magic wand and protective shield wrapped up in one. I'm not stupid, I know it's just an old belt, and I don't for a second believe in magic. But when I wrap it around my waist I feel a little bit braver.

Bravery

Monday starts off like every other Monday morning, except that Benji is still at home recovering, my mother is in London with tubes in her arms and I'm walking to school with Mattie Cohen.

"I'm so excited, aren't you excited? I mean, I'm nervous, but I'm so excited!"

Mattie is what you call a morning person. Being around her this early is so exhausting it makes me want to crawl back into bed for another two hours.

"Maybe we shouldn't walk to school together," I suggest.

Mattie stops bouncing and pouts.

"Why not?"

"We never walk to school together, it might look suspicious."

"Maybe if we talk about schoolwork?"

And so, for the rest of the walk, Mattie and I have a very lively conversation about the Louis Riel trial and whether or not he should have been hanged. When we arrive at school, she runs off to join Amanda and Min and I sit on the front steps waiting for the bell to ring. I scan the playground and see Michael leaning on the wall near the basketball court, right next to Terry. I take a deep breath and as my stomach expands it presses against Dorothy's Magic Belt, cinched around my waist, hidden underneath my stripy shirt and fleece pullover, where only I know it's there.

***

At break, Michael Greenblat shows up at my locker. He clears his throat and says, "Hey Clarissa, I made a copy of that song you wanted."

I smile and take the CD from him, like it's the most normal thing in the world.

"Oh, thanks Michael."

"No big deal."

He stands there a moment longer than is necessary before saying, "Well, I better get my stuff for gym. See you in class."

"See you."

I wave and tuck the CD into the zippered pocket inside my backpack, trying not to think about the split second when our hands touched.

***

Twenty minutes into a basketball game in gym class, I fall dramatically to my knees. Ms Gillespie blows the whistle and the game comes to a halt around me. Mattie is the first one by my side. She plants a hand on my forehead and clucks her tongue.

"Her forehead's all hot and sweaty — I think she has a fever," she announces.

Ms Gillespie frowns.

"What's wrong, Clarissa? Did you feel okay this morning?"

I moan and shake my head.

"I had a headache but I thought I would be fine. I guess I was wrong."

"She should go to the nurse, Ms Gillespie. What if she faints?"

Ms Gillespie considers this.

"Or," Mattie continues, "she could be contagious!"

I heave like I might throw up and clamp my hand over my mouth. A group of people step back.

"Gross," someone mutters.

"Fine. Mattie, make sure she gets there okay."

"Yes, Ms Gillespie."

Mattie helps me to my feet and I throw an arm over her shoulder and let her drag me to the door. Once we're out of sight, Mattie giggles.

"I was so nervous, I almost threw up," she says.

I roll my eyes. Amateur.

"Come on, we don't have much time!" I grab her hand and we run soundlessly through the halls, careful to duck down in front of the classroom doors so no one sees us breaking the no-running-in-the-hallway rule. Not to mention the no-skipping-class rule. But even superheroes break the rules sometimes, and we are no longer Mattie Cohen and Clarissa Delaney, measly seventh-grade students. We are the Matador and the Emerald Eagle, and we are unstoppable.

***

Mattie sits down outside the radio station. She's brought her binder to make it look like she's studying in the hall. If I hear her whistle the first few bars of O Canada, it means someone is coming and I need to hide. I look both ways down the hall and once at Mattie, who gives me a thumbs up, before I slip inside.

"What are you doing here?"

I practically jump right out of my skin. Jessica Riley is already in there, sucking on a lozenge and gargling with water. She insists it helps limber up her voice and make it "radio ready."

"What are you doing here?" she repeats, frowning at my sweaty gym clothes.

Be brave, I tell myself. You are the Emerald Eagle. Think of the less fortunate citizens of Ferndale. Think of Benji!

"I—I forgot to hand in today's segment."

I take the CD, labelled *Things You Don't Know About Ferndale, Part IV*, from my backpack. The letters are still fresh, the ink barely dry. I smudged the T on *Things* with my thumb. I hope she doesn't notice.

"Cutting it a little close, aren't we?" Jessica says. "Honestly, I can't believe Mr. Campbell would leave something as important as the radio station in your hands."

She opens a drawer under the soundboard.

"All the segments are kept in here," she says.

I squeeze past her and flip through the CDs as she starts shouting out vowel sounds. She sounds like a dying cow or a barking seal, I can't decide which. A-ha! Here it is. I toss my hair over one shoulder, checking to see that Jessica isn't watching. She isn't. I switch the original CD for the fake CD that Michael gave me and make my way to the door.

"Have a good show, Jessica. You sound great."

Jessica glares at me as I slip out the door. Mattie springs to her feet.

"I heard voices!" she hisses.

I grab her wrist and pull her down the hall.

"Jessica was there—"

"What?"

"Don't worry, I got it. It's fine. But it was a close one."

"I can't take much more of this superhero stuff," Mattie says.

"Don't worry Matador, we're practically home-free."

***

By the time we make it to the cafeteria, I am completely out of breath and too nervous to eat any of my lunch.

"Gooooood afternoon Ferndale! You're listening to the Lunchtime Lineup! I'm Jessica Riley, and the rest of the Radio Ferndale crew and I want to give your meal a little flavour! Next up, part four in the six-part series, 'Things You Didn't Know About Ferndale.'"

At first people keep talking; they're yelling over the PA and mimicking Jessica Riley's phoney announcer voice. The novelty of having our own radio station wore off long ago. But as the segment begins, and people recognize the voice and start to realize that this isn't your typical broadcast, a hush falls over the lunch room.

"Are you kidding me? Jason Armstrong couldn't have done it if you paid him a million dollars. He doesn't have the guts; he just does what I tell him to. I'm the one who beat the snot out of that kid. Everyone knows it: they just know better than to go runnin' to Donner. Kid's got my handiwork printed all over his sorry little face."

Terry's voice rings through the silence, echoing in every nook and cranny of the caf. The teacher on lunch duty is having a fit, trying to page the office and turn down the volume on the PA system at the same time. Mattie reaches for my hand under the table and squeezes it tightly.

Next comes Michael's voice, a little muffled, but understandable.

"Aren't you even a little sorry? He was in the hospital and everything."

"Well, serves him right for ratting me out. No one rats out Terry DiCarlo. Plus, he's not normal, you know? Hell, you ever see him hanging out with other guys, doing normal things?

No. He doesn't have any friends, just that girl, the psycho with the smart mouth, the tall one. What's her name?"

"Clarissa."

It feels strange to hear my name over the PA. A chill runs down my back and I feel the eyes of the whole cafeteria staring at me.

"Well, whatever her name is, she's got a mouth on her. She'd better watch her back, otherwise I'll cream her, too. I don't care if she's a girl."

Michael says something, but I can't make out the words. Then Terry's voice is back.

"What's your problem? Is she your girlfriend? Or wait, maybe you're in love with him. Is that it? What's the matter, did I put your little boyfriend in the hospital? Is that what this is about? I'm sick of looking at you. Get out of here."

No one speaks. After a second, Jessica Riley's perky voice comes back on, blabbing away about March Break and the school play. She's talking even faster than normal. A swarm of people huddle around Michael's table. They recognized his voice and are grilling him with questions. He looks up and catches my eye for a second before turning away and shrugging off their questions, like it's no big deal. A surge of feeling, not quite love, rushes through my heart for Michael Greenblat. Brave, dependable, floppy-haired Michael Greenblat.

"We did it!"

Mattie is at my elbow, squealing in my ear. I can smell the strawberry yogurt on her breath.

"I can't believe we did it!"

Boo-yeah!

"Clarissa, when I asked you to assist in the radio room, this is not quite what I had in mind."

For the second time in a week I am sitting at my desk after class, facing off with Mr. Campbell. But this time no amount of lecturing can make me feel bad about what I've done. What Mattie and Michael and I have done. The Terrific Trio, the Triumphant Three. No matter what the administration does to me, I have righted a wrong and liberated Ferndale Public School from fear. Mattie told almost the entire school that I masterminded the whole thing, that I switched the discs before lunch. There is a whole group of people waiting for me in the playground, ready to jump to my defence if Terry or one of his friends shows up. I am a martyr, willing to die for my cause.

"If you want me to say I'm sorry then you can just go ahead and give me detention or suspend me or whatever," I say bravely. "Because I am not even the littlest bit sorry."

Mr. Campbell looks amused.

"Clarissa, I'm not going to suspend you. Despite your methods being slightly, shall we say, unorthodox, technically you didn't break any rules."

I try not to smirk. That was the beauty of The Plan. It was all perfectly legit. As media assistant it was my job to gather and deliver interesting segments for the Lunchtime Lineup. Mission accomplished.

"I just wish you had come to me or another teacher first."

When I don't say anything, Mr. Campbell continues.

"The school has a zero-tolerance policy on bullying. If you or Benji had come to me earlier, I could have helped earlier."

I snort in spite of myself.

"How?"

"There are steps we can take in these situations."

"You would've just made it worse! Whenever teachers are involved it just gets worse. Terry would have been even madder."

"I imagine he's pretty angry right now."

"But at least I'm not a snitch, not technically. If he hadn't been bragging about it he never would have been caught, so it's his own fault."

Mr. Campbell raises his hands to show me that he means no offence.

"I'm not disagreeing with you, Clarissa. I won't even pretend to understand the finer points of middle-school justice. I just want you to know that you don't have to take on a bully by yourself."

"I wasn't by myself."

Mr. Campbell raises his eyebrows but doesn't ask me to name my accomplices. Obviously Michael has already been questioned and owned up to his involvement. He said he was proud to be a part of the plan. Mattie asked me to keep her name out of it. I figure it's the least I can do.

"Very well. In the future, please keep me informed of any problems. Now, I'm afraid I'm going to have to take back the keys to the radio room. As much as I admire your courage, I can't support vigilante justice."

I'm not entirely certain what he means, but I know I'm not being punished and that's all that matters. I stand.

"May I go now?"

"You may."

Outside, Mattie, Michael and a bunch of other kids from class are hanging around on the swings, waiting for me. They jump up as I exit the classroom.

"Well?" Mattie demands.

"Well, nothing. I'm free!"

Mattie pumps her fist in the air and squeals, "Justice!" The other kids whoop and cheer and I smile so hard my cheeks hurt.

***

"And that's it?" Benji asks. "No detention, no extra credit?"

"Nothing!" I chirp. "And when you come back, no Terry DiCarlo! He's been expelled!"

Benji smiles. His bruises have turned from purple to green to yellow and the cut on his lip has healed. He's not exactly what you'd call the picture of health, but Benji never was a rosy kid.

"So when are you coming back to school? Tomorrow?"

"Maybe," Benji says.

"You can't stay in bed forever," I point out. "Plus, Michael said he'd look out for you."

Benji grins. "Michael said?"

I blush furiously.

"It's a nice thing to do!" I snap.

"Have you been hanging out?"

"No, he just helped out with The Plan. It's not like we eat lunch together or walk home together after school."

"Yet," Benji says.

But before he can add anything else I nail him with a pillow. He's not so banged up that he can't take a little feather action.

Blessed

"Where's the juice?"

"You told me to bring food," Mattie protests.

"I told you to bring *refreshments*," I clarify.

Mattie is indignant. "That's what I did," she pouts. "I made the cookies special! I even put an A for Annie on them in M&M's."

"I didn't ask you to make As, I asked you to bring *refreshments* and refreshments include drinks!"

"Well, I'm sorry but you didn't specify drinks."

Great. The guests have all arrived, Mom and Denise will be here any minute and there is nothing to drink.

"There's some apple juice in the fridge," Benji says.

Mattie looks dismayed. "That's it?"

I open the fridge and scour the shelves.

"That's it," I confirm. "It'll have to do."

Honestly. What kind of hostess has nothing to offer her guests in the way of drinks? The cookies were Mattie's idea, but the surprise party was mine. Mom is coming home from Hopestead and I wanted to give her a royal welcome. Denise invited some of Mom's friends and her favourite clients. I invited Mattie, Benji and Michael.

Benji looks as good as new. He brought a bouquet of

daffodils and a card he made himself, with Mom dressed up as a superhero. Mattie brought a cookie sheet. "So you can bake together," she said brightly. Poor Mattie. She means well but she sure doesn't know Annie Delaney.

The doorbell rings and I open it to find Michael in a buttoned-up shirt and his hair parted, like he's on his way to church or something. "Hi, Clarissa." He thrusts an enormous bouquet wrapped in silver paper between us. "These are for your mom."

I thank him and take it into the kitchen with the others. There are so many bouquets in the house, it feels like I'm living in the middle of a garden. We're running out of things to put them in. I improvise by cutting off the top of a pop bottle and filling it with water. It's Mattie's idea. Thank goodness she's really into arts and crafts.

I hear the car pull into the driveway before I see it. Benji does, too. He's been listening for our car for years. We make eye contact and start shushing people. There really isn't anywhere to hide, so people just shuffle to one side of the room.

The door opens.

"We're back," Denise calls. I hear the sound of bags hitting the floor and keys being tossed onto the counter. "Clarissa? Where are you?"

"In the living room!" I call back, just like we planned, like it's normal for me to just hang out on my own in the living room. If there is one flaw in the plan, this is it.

When Mom comes around the corner, everyone yells, "Surprise!" and then someone starts singing "Happy Birthday."

I hear Mattie shush them, hissing, "It's a welcome home party, not her birthday."

If Mom notices, she doesn't let on. She's smiling from ear to ear. Denise gives her a quick squeeze and a big noisy kiss on the cheek.

"Welcome home, Annie, we missed you." She gestures at mom's loyal fans, spread out across the living room. "We all missed you."

Mom starts making her way through the crowd, always the Dairy Queen, shaking hands, hugging and laughing. I hang back to watch her. She's too skinny and there are bags under her eyes that never used to be there. I'm relieved to see she still has her hair, even though I know that some-day soon that might not be the case. She's had it cut so it lands in a neat bob around her ears. It makes her chin look pointier and her eyes seem bigger. Even so, she's still the most beautiful person in the room.

Benji gives her the card he made. His hands shake a little and I know he's holding back tears.

"Bless you, you've given me a tinier waist and better cleav-age," she says, pulling him into a big hug. Unfortunately she says this in front of Michael, who turns even redder than I do. I catch his eye and shrug, as if to say, what can you do, and he shrugs back. Now I'm really blushing.

Mattie marches over and offers her hand, introducing her-self as, "Cheryl Cohen's daughter and a friend of Clarissa's."

"And where is that lovely daughter of mine?" Mom asks.

I step forward, feeling shy in front of all these people.

"Welcome home," I say.

Mom wraps me in a bear hug and kisses my hair, whis-pering all sorts of embarrassing baby talk into my almost-curls. Only today I don't mind so much. I hug her back with all my might and I don't care who sees.

The party is a roaring success. My cheeks hurt from all the smiling I'm doing. Everything is going perfectly to plan, well, except for the apple juice fiasco, until the doorbell rings and Denise walks into the room with Mr. Campbell at her side.

I can't help myself. "Who invited Tony the Tiger?" I say.

"I received lovely invitation from a Miss Denise Renzetti," Mr. Campbell answers. Note to self: kill Denise.

"I couldn't resist the opportunity to welcome home the famous Annette Delaney," Mr. Campbell continues, shaking my mother's hand and bowing slightly. She looks totally charmed.

"Mr. Campbell, thank you for coming. You are a hot topic of conversation around this house."

"I can only imagine," he says. For a terrible minute I worry that he told Mom about the letters, but then he winks at me and I feel better. It's still our secret. As goofy and lame as he is, Tony the Tiger can keep a secret.

He gives Mom a book, something inspirational, along with a bag of loose tea that is supposed to help you sleep.

"My sister swears by the stuff," he says.

Mom accepts it graciously.

"There's also something I've been meaning to give you, Clarissa." Mr. Campbell says.

"Me?" I ask. "What is it?"

I wrack my brains trying to come up with what it could be. Did I forget my lunch bag at school? Or an assignment? But what Mr. Campbell has to show me isn't even close.

"I found it at the back of my desk. Someone must have lost it. Who knows how long it's been hiding there."

Mr. Campbell fishes around in his pocket and pulls out a single earring, slim, silver, in the shape of a feather. My breath catches in my throat. It's the same earring Miss Ross was wearing that day in her classroom. I'm sure of it.

"Well isn't that pretty," Mom says. "We can get a little jump ring and you can put it on a chain, like a necklace."

Mattie grins at me from across the room. I know what

she's thinking. "Your talisman," she mouths before making flapping motions with her arms. Benji looks at her like she's crazy and she pulls him aside and starts at the beginning. "Every superhero needs a talisman . . ."

Mr. Campbell is smiling at me and I am surprised to feel myself grinning back. When I am able to find my voice again, I manage to squeak out a thank you that sounds genuine.

He gives a little bow. "You are very welcome," he says. "When I found it, a little voice in my head kept saying, 'Give me to Clarissa,' and I have discovered, in the past, that it is wise to listen to the voices in your head."

"That's not what my doctor says," Denise cracks and, for once, everyone laughs along with her.

He may not be Miss Ross, or even close to it, but Mr. Campbell is starting to grow on me. I bet there aren't many teachers who would give a kid like me so many chances. For this reason I decide to forgive Mr. Campbell for his bad jokes and terrible clothes and the fact that he will never be Miss Ross. Thanks to him, I have one last little piece of her, something I can wear close to my heart and remind me to be a better person.

"A toast," Mom says, raising her apple juice high. "To my daughter Clarissa, who is tough as nails and keeps everyone laughing with that wonderful sense of humour, even while babysitting my best friend Denise while I was gone—"

"Watch it, Annie!" Denise swats her lightly on the arm.

"—and who brought all of us together for this wonderful shindig. To Clarissa!"

"To Clarissa!"

My ears are ringing with the sound of my own name, spoken by a roomful of smiling people. I feel light and airy and ready to take on whatever the universe wants to throw at me. If you told me a year ago that I'd be standing in the middle of a surprise party that I planned with Mattie Cohen and Michael Greenblat, I would have told you to get lost, or at the very least, get medical help, because you were seriously crazy. I guess it's true that you can't predict the future, and all you can do is make a wish, hope for the best and deal with whatever the universe throws at you. But it's nice to know that there are days, like today, where everything just clicks. And that sometimes, just sometimes, the universe is listening.

Acknowledgments

There aren't enough words (B or otherwise) to express my deep gratitude to the many people who have encouraged me to realize a life-long dream of becoming a published author. I am grateful for all of my friends and family who amaze and inspire me in writing and in life. Very special thanks to everyone at Scholastic Canada, Cathy Francis, Nina McCreath, Elaine Cowan, Patti Thorlakson, Ashley Benson, Rob Kempson, Rebecca Jess, Denise Anderson, Jennifer MacKinnon, and especially to Kallie George, without whom I never would have finished this novel. Love, love, love.